"Then I'll talk t⟨ ⟩ allow you to continue to profit on the use my property. With a firm nod, the woman stormed out.

Colt could swear he felt the breeze from the swinging doors as they moved back and forth for several seconds. "Well, that was interesting." He took another sip of his tea.

"Do you think she'll be back?" Canna asked.

"Absolutely. That woman has more steam than a locomotive. She's convinced she's in the right. There's no stopping a woman when she's in such a state."

He finished his tea and handed Hanson the glass. No sense setting it down. Hanson would snatch it up and wash it within two blinks of an eye.

Colt had paused on the balcony before coming down and almost chuckled at the memory of the look on Hanson's face. The quiet bartender had been thrown for a loop by Mrs. Baker. It wasn't every day The Golden Lady got her type of visitor.

With his thumb hanging in his vest pocket, Colt leaned one elbow on the bar, just as casual as could be, and thought about the widow.

She was pretty, in an odd little bird sort of way, but very attractive, with the exception of her choice in hairstyles. Her light brown hair twisted up into some sort of bun he could only assume she thought was proper for a widow, did not look good on the woman.

But those eyes. They made him pause. Her widow's weeds gone, the soft blue dress she wore accentuated her sky-blue eyes, and they seemed to look right into his soul.

A Woman of Means

By

Jo Barrett

A Woman of Means
COPYRIGHT © 2022 by Jo Barrett

Contact Information: info@thewildrosepress.com
Cover Art by *The Wild Rose Press, Inc.*
The Wild Rose Press, Inc.
PO Box 708
Adams Basin, NY 14410-0708
Visit us at www.thewildrosepress.com

Publishing History
First Edition, 2022
Trade Paperback ISBN 978-1-5092-4391-4
Digital ISBN 978-1-5092-4392-1

Published in the United States of America

Prologue

New York, New York 1875

There's no reason to stay, Hattie thought, as she looked about the luxurious house she'd grown up in. When her husband went off to perform some sort of survey work, determined to get as far away from her as possible, she'd moved back in so she could take care of her father and to not be alone. But now, with her father gone these last six months, it no longer felt like home. And with her husband dead, killed in some fight over a game of cards, or so the note along with his personal possessions she'd received said, there was no reason to move back to the house he'd purchased when they wed.

"As if I would," she said.

He'd traveled all over the country for his work, and never came home. Not even once over the course of five years, which was perfectly fine with her. At least he'd not pestered her father for funds too often, so he somehow managed to pay his way. But he'd never sent a penny to support her or pay for their home. As far as he was concerned, she was her father's responsibility.

"Reprobate", she muttered, rising from her chair.

She shook her head at the intensity of her own words. It was said one shouldn't speak ill of the dead, so the less she thought of John Baker the better.

Looking about the room once more, forcing her

husband from her thoughts, new tears came to her eyes. She would miss the long talks she often had with her father by the fire, the slight twinkle in his eye when he was telling one of his tall tales to make her smile. But he'd been in pain for so very long, longer than she'd ever suspected. She hated having to hear from their family doctor how poor his health was after he'd passed, but Father had sworn the man to secrecy. He hadn't wanted her to worry and fret over something she could not control. It was so like him to do that. She'd never known a kinder man and she adored him. But she had to accept that he was gone, finally at peace alongside her mother.

"Mrs. Baker, would you like a cup of tea?" the maid asked, stepping into the ornate parlor.

Startled and yet relieved by the intrusion, she pushed aside the sadness building inside her at the loss. "Thank you, Mary, but no." She relaxed her shoulders, easing their tenseness and swiped the last of her tears away and turned. "I think what I do need, however, is a good many crates and boxes."

"Ma'am?"

"I'm selling it all, Mary. Whatever isn't of family importance or sentimental to me personally in some way goes."

The shock on the maid's face was quite plain, and Hattie could only assume that it was due to the uncertainty of the woman's future employment, rather than what Hattie was about to do. The rest of the staff would be quite surprised as well, but she had made up her mind.

"But—but the house too, ma'am?"

"All of it." She crossed to the maid, and clasped the maid's shaking hands gently. "Mary, I will not toss you and the rest of the staff out. I will see to it personally that you all have gainful employment before I am done. This I promise you. But where I'm going, I won't need any staff."

"Where are you going, ma'am?"

Hattie grinned. "West, Mary. I'm going west."

Chapter One

Hattie stepped off the train and onto the platform, grateful for the respite from the uncomfortable seating. "Well Father, that is one lesson learned the hard way," she whispered to herself.

He'd always told her traveling should be done in comfort and to never skimp on accommodations. He'd done quite a lot of it, and now she understood what he meant. From this moment on, she would take a Pullman car and damn the expense.

It wasn't as if she was a pauper. He'd provided for her very well after his death, as opposed to her husband who had left her a saloon, of all things. And she had the money from the sale of the house and those things she could make herself part with to see her through. But she had no real idea of what condition the saloon was in, and didn't want to squander any of her funds if it wasn't necessary.

Willow Bend, Wyoming was a little larger than she'd imagined, but most of the towns on the train schedule were growing so rapidly it wasn't any wonder it was more than just a crossroads. She hoped this would bode well for her idea about the old saloon.

With the ownership of it passing to her after her husband's death more than a year ago, she could only venture to guess it was still in good condition. Filthy, no doubt, with heaven knew what hiding in the corners and beneath the floorboards, but she was its new owner, and was determined to make it hers in every way possible.

Her trunk and valise were unloaded along with several crates of goods, no doubt to be delivered to the general store, at the other end of the platform. She spied a young man taking note of the crates, and made her way toward him.

"Excuse me," she said. "I'd like to arrange to have my trunk delivered to the hotel."

"I can do that, ma'am. I just need to make sure I don't miss one of these shipments. The boss would have my hide."

"I understand." Waiting a few more moments while he finished his cataloging, she took note of his age, finding him much younger than she'd assumed. But he seemed a decent sort, intent on doing a good job. It was difficult not to smile at how hard he was concentrating on his task, as his tongue would slip to the corner of his lips while he wrote the names on a slate.

"Okay, I reckon I got'em all. Now which of these is yours, ma'am?"

"The large one there. I'll take the small valise with me."

"Your name, ma'am?"

"Mrs. John Baker."

He mouthed her name as he inspected the trunk. "Alright, ma'am. I'll make sure this gets to the hotel. Should be no more than an hour."

"Thank you, Mr.—"

He chuckled with a blush. "No one ever called me a mister. It's just Jeremy, ma'am. Jeremy Davis."

"Well, thank you." She handed him several coins.

"Oh, this is too much Mrs. Baker. Deliverin' trunks

is part of the job."

She clasped her hand over his, closing his fist around the coins. "A job I believe you are very good at—Mr. Davis."

With a smile, she turned, picked up her valise and started toward the hotel, roughly two blocks away. The young man was unaware how heavy her trunk was, and will have surely earned the tip by the time it reached the hotel. And as her father had taught her, always appreciate a hard worker, and the best way was with a smile, a few coins, and a heartfelt thank you.

The walk was pleasant, and she paused at a few of the shops along the way to gaze into the windows. In fact, the more she saw of Willow Bend, the more she liked it. It was growing by leaps and bounds, and had a variety of businesses, which meant a variety of customers.

Her hopes to turn the old saloon into an upscale restaurant sounded more feasible with every step. She'd done her research. The only restaurant of any kind was the one in the hotel. And with the number of people moving west, and the rate at which the town was growing, it should be able to support such an endeavor.

She paused as she eyed the hotel across the street. At least she hoped it could support two eating establishments. The hotel restaurant did appear to be quite large.

"But they don't have me as their cook," she muttered under her breath, then crossed the street.

If Hattie was anything other than punctual and a good businesswoman, she was an excellent cook. She prided herself on her confectionary talents, but she never had a dissatisfied guest at her table. It was one of the few compliments her husband had ever given her. That and her looks. He seemed to think she was passable pretty.

She shook off the memory of him and entered the hotel.

A man behind the counter lifted his head from a stack of mail in his hands, and set it aside. "Good morning, ma'am."

"Good morning." She set her valise on the floor at her feet. "I am Mrs. Baker. I made a reservation by wire earlier this week."

"Oh yes, Mrs. Baker. We're very happy to have you with us." He spun the guest book around for her to sign. "I have your room ready for you as you requested."

"Thank you." She signed the register and paid him in advance for the night. She wasn't sure if the saloon was in any condition for habitation, and had made arrangements to pay in advance for each night she required her room. "Is the dining room still open for breakfast?"

"No ma'am, but if you're hungry, I could see if my wife can make you some toast or something and send it to your room."

"That's very kind of you, but no thank you. I'll just wait until lunch."

He handed her the key. "You're in number fifteen. It's straight up the stairs and near the end of the all on the left."

"Thank you. And could you also direct me to The Golden Lady Saloon?"

He blinked a moment, his brows disappearing beneath the thin oiled hair swept across his forehead. "Um, the saloon, you said?"

"Yes, The Golden Lady?" She wasn't about to give

the man any explanations and she couldn't very well explain her purpose for seeing the saloon. The last thing she needed to do was to tip off the competition about her plans. After all, it was none of his business that she'd become the new owner of the saloon upon her husband's death.

"Um, well, it's two blocks down the street, just past the bend in the road on the right. You can't miss it."

"Thank you." With that she lifted her valise and climbed the stairs to her room.

****

Refreshed from her travels, Hattie made her way out of the hotel and down the street to the saloon, only to find that it was in full operation. Although it was early in the day, barely ten o'clock, the batwing doors were open and a young boy was sweeping the walk in front of the doors. The windows all seemed moderately clean, while the signage in good if not perfect condition. There was no sign of neglect whatsoever.

Somewhat flummoxed by the site, she took a deep breath, threw back her shoulders and marched across the street just as the young man slipped back inside. Someone had obviously taken advantage of the empty saloon and claimed it as their own. It was the only explanation. A mistake that was soon to be rectified.

She paused at the doors and peered inside. There were no customers as of yet, only the boy and a bartender cleaning a glass. A large mirror banked the wall behind the bar, but a painting of questionable taste hung above it. The brass boot rest was in need of polishing and the floors, although swept, needed a good scrubbing. The wood surrounding the bar itself could use a good waxing as well, as it appeared rather dingy. Still, all in all the saloon was in excellent condition, considering what she expected.

With a false sense of bravado, she pushed through the doors and walked up to the bar.

"Excuse me. Can you tell me who is in charge here?"

The bartender stopped rubbing the beer glass and looked at her with slightly wide eyes, while the boy froze in mid-sweep, peering at her from beneath a mess of unkempt hair and a dingy old hat.

"Um, that would be Colt. Mr. Coltrane, I mean," the bartender said.

"I'd like to speak with him, please."

"Um, well, ma'am, he's likely not awake yet."

"He's up," the boy said. "Heard him grumbling around in the kitchen a half hour ago."

The bartender glanced at the boy and gave him half a nod, sending the child running up the stairs.

"Canna will fetch him, ma'am."

"Thank you."

He resumed his cleaning of the glass. "Could I offer you some water or something, ma'am?"

"No thank you, Mr…"

"Hanson, ma'am. George Hanson."

"Have you been working her for very long, Mr. Hanson?"

"Yes, ma'am. I've been here for about three years."

"I see. And how long has this Mr. Coltrane been in charge?"

Movement on the stairs, reflected in the mirror behind the bar, caught her attention. The man was well dressed in what she assumed to be gambler garb. A red and gold embroidered vest, dark suit, string tie, and dangerously dark looks.

She blinked a moment, mentally setting aside the physical effects of his handsome visage on her person, and turned.

He stepped off the last stair and moved across the room. "Not that it's any of your business, but I've been owner here for six months."

"Mr. Coltrane, I presume?"

He gave a terse nod.

"Well, Mr. Coltrane, you're trespassing."

He slowly crossed to where she stood at the bar. "Excuse me?"

"Trespassing. I am the owner of this saloon. I inherited it over a year ago."

"Is that so?"

"Yes, and I have the paperwork to prove it."

"And I have paperwork to prove I'm the owner." He motioned to Mr. Hanson to poor him a drink, of what she couldn't be sure, but she suspected it wasn't liquor. That made her pause, as it had the color of it, but it clearly came from a pitcher and not a bottle.

She tossed away her silly notions of what a gambler may or may not drink in the morning and returned to the matter at hand. "Clearly you cannot be the owner since you only took possession six months ago," she said. "At that time, it would have already belonged to me. And I did not sell the property."

"So who died?" He lifted his drink to his lips while studying her over his glass.

She stiffened her spine and gave him a bit of a scowl, not liking his glib attitude.

"It's obvious you're not the type to intentionally purchase a saloon," he remarked with a smug grin.

"Very well. My husband."

He let out a sigh as he set the glass on the bar. "Sorry for your loss. However, that still doesn't prove you're the owner. Your husband was likely swindled."

"I believe it was you who were swindled, Mr. Coltrane."

"Then we are at an impasse, Mrs. Baker."

She refrained from cursing beneath her breath. She'd not expected this type of encumbrance. "Very well, I shall retain a lawyer immediately and we'll settle this in court." With that, she spun around and made her way to the batwing doors.

"The only lawyer in town is currently doing his rounds around the territory," he said. "It's going to be at least two weeks before he gets back. I suggest you go home and rethink this whole thing."

She paused, tossed a scowl at him over her shoulder and said, "Then I'll talk to the sheriff, because I refuse to allow you to continue to profit off the use my property." With a firm nod, she stormed out.

Colt could swear he felt the breeze from the swinging doors as they moved back and forth for several seconds. "Well, that was interesting." He took another sip of his tea.

"Do you think she'll be back?" Canna asked.

"Absolutely. That woman has more steam than a locomotive. She's convinced she's in the right. There's no stopping a woman when she's in such a state."

He finished his tea and handed Hanson the glass. No sense setting it down. Hanson would snatch it up and wash it within two blinks of an eye.

Colt had paused on the balcony before coming down and almost chuckled at the memory of the look on

Hanson's face. The quiet bartender had been thrown for a loop by Mrs. Baker. It wasn't every day The Golden Lady got her type of visitor.

With his thumb hanging in his vest pocket, Colt leaned one elbow on the bar, just as casual as could be, and thought about the widow.

She was pretty, in an odd little bird sort of way, but very attractive, with the exception of her choice in hairstyles. Her light brown hair twisted up into some sort of bun he could only assume she thought was proper for a widow, did not look good on the woman.

But those eyes. They made him pause. Her widow's weeds gone, the soft blue dress she wore accentuated her sky-blue eyes, and they seemed to look right into his soul.

Odd that she didn't come off as one of those snooty old bitty types he would expect from someone of her quality. She seemed affable, with the exception of the current situation. Her color ran hot in her cheeks when she was riled, but that only made her all the more appealing. Still, she had to have a screw loose to want to take possession of a saloon.

Canna moved to the window and studied the street in the direction of the sheriff's office. "Looks like she's got money."

"Yep," Colt replied. "Which makes her wanting this place all the more unusual." He kept his thoughts on her sanity to himself. Someone of her ilk would never walk into a saloon, much less claim to own one.

"She's from back east, ain't she? All them ladies dress like that back there, don't they Colt?"

He gave the kid a nod, noting Canna's intense interest. Could be the kid was afraid Colt would let the lady have the saloon, and the kid would be without a home and a job. Or could be, Mrs. Baker was the first lady Canna had ever seen. Most likely it was a bit of both. They had ladies in Willow Bend, but none from the upper classes.

It wouldn't be long before the woman returned with Matt in tow. The sheriff was a friend and honest to a fault. And a lady in distress wouldn't be something he'd ignore. Especially not a lady of such obvious quality.

"Yup, here they come," Canna said. The kid went back to sweeping the floor, but Colt knew all ears, the kid's and Hanson's were set to catch everything that happened next. He couldn't really blame them. Their jobs were potentially on the line, even though he was certain he was the rightful and soul owner of The Golden Lady.

Matt pushed open one of the doors and ushered Mrs. Baker through.

"Mornin' Colt."

"Matt," Colt said with a nod. "Care for a drink?"

"No thanks, too early and I got a pot of coffee waitin' on me back at the office."

"So, what can I do for you, Matt?" He felt silly asking, but knew the cordialities would ruffle the lady's feathers and just couldn't resist. He did enjoy the sight of her flushed cheeks.

"Well it's like this. Seems the widow here has a claim to the saloon. I seen the paper, so I can't outright ignore it."

"And I have one of the same, as you know."

The sheriff tipped his hat back off his forehead. "Yeah, I know, but I think you two need to talk this out, seein' as how Mrs. Baker can't get any legal representation right now."

Colt sighed, knowing it was useless to argue the point. "Fine. Come with me and we'll compare notes in my office."

The widow lifted her chin and followed him through a door in the back of the saloon, then he ushered her and Matt down a long hallway.

He walked toward an open door half-way down and motioned for them to enter.

"Please take a seat, Mrs. Baker," he said, and crossed to the bookcase along the outer wall.

As she settled herself in one of the large leather studded chairs across from his massive mahogany desk, the sheriff moved to stand behind the second. He leaned his forearms along its high back. They both watched as Colt pulled open a false set of shelves from the wall where a large safe hid tucked behind. Matt knew the safe was there, and Colt didn't think it necessary to hide its location from the lady. It probably wasn't a secret to anyone in town anyway. Just one of old man Cofield's eccentricities.

Colt retrieved his bill of sale from the safe then crossed to Mrs. Baker and handed it to her. "As you can see, madam, I am the owner of The Golden Lady."

A lone brow rose with a small smirk teasing at the corner of her lips. She then pulled her bill of sale from her reticule.

"And here is mine, Mr. Coltrane."

He took her slip of paper then went around the desk and sat down. After a few moments of looking over the document, he said, "Mrs. Baker it would seem we have a dilemma. Old man Cofield, the owner of this saloon, had a partner at one time, George Poole. It had been reported that he was killed in the war, leaving Cofield the saloon in its entirety. Your bill of sale is for Poole's portion, while mine is for Cofield's."

The odd little bird, whose back was ramrod straight, gave him a look that had him adjusting his initial impression of her. This was no loony female. There was a keen mind behind those big blue eyes, which was another mark in her favor—a list of attributes he'd best be ignoring before he got himself into trouble.

"Then, Mr. Coltrane, it would appear we are partners in this endeavor," she said.

Her words, steady and sure, validated Colt's quick re-appraisal, and slapped a little cold water on where his mind kept wanting to wander.

"That's possible, but I think first we need to determine if your bill of sale is valid. A dead man can't sell his property. Or in your case, lose it in a card game."

She nodded, her pink lips somewhat pursed in thought. "I agree. We need to determine the validity of the transaction. Of mine and of yours."

"Well, Mrs. Baker, mine was witnessed by Matt here." Colt waved a hand toward the sheriff. "He saw me win the saloon from old man Cofield himself. So I daresay that transaction is valid, wouldn't you?"

She let out a soft sigh, and for a half a second, maybe even a whole second, he imagined that sigh against his lips, then mentally shook himself. Now was not the time for such thoughts. He liked it in Willow Bend, and he liked his saloon. He didn't want to make a mistake by letting a pretty little widow sway him in handing the whole thing over.

He'd done enough traveling, played all the big poker games, and seen enough of the country. He was tired and ready to settle down in one place, play poker at his leisure, and just live life. This woman could jeopardize his plans. She'd said it herself, she hadn't expected the saloon to be in operation. That meant she had other plans for The Golden Lady, and he was sure that none of those plans included gambling and drinking.

"Well then, if Mr. Poole is dead, then there should be a record of it somewhere. Then the date of his death and the date of my bill of sale can then be compared," she said.

Colt looked to Matt. "Any paperwork at your place, Matt?"

He shook his head. "Nope. I think Cofield got a telegram, but it was before my time."

"Then gentlemen, we'll need to contact the government," she said. "You said he was reported as killed in action during the war. They should have what we need to verify his death and subsequently my bill of sale."

"I can see what they can tell us over at the Cavalry office," Matt said. "They can tell us where to go from there to get the information we need. Probably have to send a letter to Washington. Could take months to get any kind of answer."

The woman nodded, her back still straight as a stick. "Then in that case I suggest Mr. Coltrane and I operate on the pretense that we are partners until proven otherwise."

A chill ran down Colt's spine.

"Now Mrs. Baker—"

"You cannot sway me in this, sir. I am fully aware of my legal rights."

Matt cleared an obvious chuckle from his throat.

"You may as well accept it, Colt, instead of tryin' to convince her otherwise. She'll just leave you twistin' in the wind." He straightened from his casual lean across the chair. "No sense in wastin' all that energy when you already know the outcome."

Colt nodded, knowing legally, at the moment, she owned half the saloon. He'd spent the majority of his life surrounded by the law. He was from a long line of lawyers, all highly successful, and it had been expected he would follow the same path. But that life wasn't for him. The old Wild West tales had attracted him when he was a boy, and its thrall pulled him into the life he currently lived. A life he thoroughly enjoyed. But now, a woman—a woman of quality, no less, had upended his perfect world, and it galled him to no end.

"Fine," he said, a low growl in the back of his throat. "But I think the best thing for you to do now, Mrs. Baker, is to go back home until this is settled. I will hold all profits in the bank, verified by Matt here, until things are straightened out. I'll even take you down to the bank where we can draw up an agreement on the deposits."

"I'm afraid I can't do that. I have no home to go back too. I sold my house in New York, as I intended to live here."

"In the saloon?"

"Yes, in the saloon. Of course I had assumed it was not in operation. As it stands now, it would not be proper for me to reside her, more's the pity. Therefore, I will remain at the hotel and arrive here promptly at seven in the morning to begin work."

"Work."

"Yes, work. Things people do to earn a living."

Colt bit back his grin. He really liked her spunk and

quick mind. "And what work do you intend to do, Mrs. Baker? Entertain the men?"

She cast him a scowl, and said, "I intend to take over half the duties you now perform. The duties of managing this business."

"Uh-huh. My duties."

"To be perfectly clear, Mr. Coltrane, I intend to keep an eye on my investment."

With a chuckle, Matt started for the door. "I'll leave you two to figure out the details of this here business relationship. Mrs. Baker, it has been a pleasure meetin' you." He tipped his hat to the widow, then closed the office door behind him with a soft chuckle, leaving Colt holding his aching head in his hands.

"Now, about our arrangement," she said. "I think your idea of a bank account for the deposits is a good one, but I would first like to see the books so that I might grasp the amounts expected."

"The books?"

"Yes, the books. You know ledgers—profit and loss statements—the books."

Colt sat back in his chair and closed his eyes while rubbing his forehead, a meager attempt to thwart the headache growing rapidly beneath his fingers.

"Mr. Coltrane, I realize you don't know me, and that you likely believe me to be some sort of ridiculous woman who thinks of nothing but fashion and gossip, but I assure you that is not my nature."

He peered at her from beneath his fingertips, wishing she were light a few marbles, easy to manage, but he could see that was not going to happen. Everything was going to be a battle with her, so he may as well give in to her now and save himself the trouble.

Rising from his chair, he plucked a stack of books from the shelf and plopped them on the corner of the desk before her.

"Thank you." She quickly removed her gloves, retrieved a pair of spectacles from her reticule and began to flip through the pages. All the while making small dissatisfied noises with a firm frown on her face.

Colt decided it was time for a stiff drink. He didn't care if it wasn't even eleven yet. As he poured, he shot her a glance. "If you need me to explain anything to you, just say so."

With a smirk, she looked up and began to explain the saloon's operation in great detail to him. All he could do was stare at her with his drink half-way to his lips.

"And as to these books," she continued, flipping through more of the ledgers, "they are in a sorry state. There are repeated errors, which make it difficult to determine if you're making any profit at all. There isn't even a decent tally of your inventory." She lifted her bright blue gaze to his. "You are no bookkeeper, Mr. Coltrane."

He threw back his drink, and said, "And you are?"

"Yes, I am. I managed my father's affairs for years."

"You mean the household."

"No, I mean my father's business affairs outside of his banking position. He was quite the philanthropist. He enjoyed investing in local businesses, nurturing them, and helping them succeed. In New York every neighborhood relies on the corner baker, the butcher and so on."

"I'm aware of what New York is like." He poured himself another drink.

"Ah, then you've been there."

Yeah, he'd been there, was from there, and his family still resided there. And every so often a letter would arrive from his mother or father, or even one of his brothers begging him to come home and join the law firm, which was the last thing he ever wanted to do. Representing a bunch of society snots wasn't his idea of a good life.

"Well, as you might imagine, there was always an opportunity to invest and my father never turned away from a new challenge," she said.

She put her nose back to the books, pulling him from the past, and letting the old family war fade from his mind. The problem was not the past, but the present.

"Mrs. Baker, aside from your slight at my talents at keeping the books, I propose that you take on that chore, since you appear to be so adept at it." He lifted his whiskey glass to his lips and murmured, "I only hope it doesn't cost me my shirt."

"I also have excellent hearing, Mr. Coltrane, so you need not fear for your shirt."

With a weary sigh, he set aside his unfinished drink, leaned against the credenza behind his desk, then looked her in the eye. Those damned beautiful eyes. "I think you and I need to come to an agreement on a few things."

She tipped up her chin, bracing for whatever he was about to say, and damned if that wasn't the cutest thing he'd ever seen. He almost smiled. She looked like a canary staring down the cat.

"I'm listening," she said.

He crossed his arms and gave her a stern look, although he had a feeling she wasn't easily intimated. "Neither of us will make any changes to the establishment until legal ownership has been determined."

"Define changes."

"No lace doilies on the tables. No silly fripperies decorating the bar. The painting above the bar stays, even if it upsets your sensibilities." He leaned forward, his hands planted on the desk. "And Patty and Lila stay and continue to go on as they have been."

"I agree to no changes in the décor. I will admit I dislike the painting, rather poorly done, by the way, but it doesn't upset my sensibilities. I just happen to know good—and bad art when I see it. And frankly it would be ludicrous to make any of those types of changes. This is a saloon, after all. But who are Patty and Lila? I understand your inference, but wish to be clear on the matter."

"They are saloon girls. They entertain the men, serve drinks, and whatever else they want to serve."

"I see." She sat back a moment and nibbled her bottom lip, drawing his attention to her bow-like mouth.

Damnation! To be attracted to the woman was beyond rational thought. He rubbed his brow again, although he'd rather be banging his head against the solid mahogany desk. Maybe it would knock some sense into him. He started to reach for his unfinished whiskey then thought better of it. He needed to be on his toes around Mrs. Baker, and drinking before noon was not the way to hold on to his saloon.

"Go ahead and say your peace, Mrs. Baker. I can see you have thoughts on the matter."

"Very well. Of course I don't approve of their choice of profession, but I will not say they cannot continue. I do have concerns, however, regarding the saloon taking any of their earnings for their—*services*."

Her small hand fluttered in the air as she made a distasteful face.

Her obvious discomfort over the topic made him wonder if she was one of those virgin widows. The kind that got married moments before the husband went to war, with only a quick get-the-deed-done type of consummation. Although she was far too young to be a war bride, the deed, as it were, was not a pleasant thought to her.

"What I mean to say is," she continued. "If a woman wishes to sell herself, it should be on her terms and all the proceeds hers. If Patty and Lila entertain in the main room, singing, dancing, and serving drinks, then they should be paid a wage for that. The rest, however, is none of my affair, nor should it be that of the saloon's."

Colt flopped down hard in his chair and just looked at her, stunned. "Lady, where the hell did you come from?" he muttered.

"I beg your pardon?"

He shook his head and waved off her question. "Nothing." He'd never solve the puzzle of Mrs. Baker, so he'd best stop trying and just brace himself whenever she opened her mouth, because he'd never be able to guess what went on in that pretty head of hers. "I will agree to your terms regarding the girls."

She cocked her head at him, one thin brow arched sharply. "You will?"

"Yes, I will. I never took anything from the girls anyway. Believe it or not, Mrs. Baker, it didn't seem right to me either."

"Oh. Well."

She sat back in her chair, her stiff back finally relaxed. He felt a little vindicated in that he'd thrown her for a change.

"You surprise me, Mr. Coltrane."

"Why? Because I'm a gambler?"

"No, because you're a man."

With half a chuckle, he said, "And you surprise me, Mrs. Baker."

"Because I'm a woman?"

He rose from his chair and made his way to the door. "A woman of quality." He paused and glanced back at her over his shoulder. "A rather pretty one at that."

Her cheeks flushed and she averted her gaze, all very telling. He wasn't a damn good gambler for nothing. He could read people, and although she'd had him scrambling to figure her out, she was still a woman. A woman who rarely got compliments. He wouldn't be surprised if his virgin assessment wasn't also true. How could any man not want to bring a flush to her cheeks and see the sated look in her eyes after bedding her?

Damn it to Hell! He needed to read her, not want her!

He yanked open the door and stuck his head out. "Canna! Bring coffee! And lots of it!" He turned to the wide blue-eyed gaze of his tormentor, then stuck his head back out the door. "Two cups!"

Chapter Two

Hattie tried to hide her grin, but knew she failed. She liked this man, although she couldn't really say why. He was devilishly handsome, and surprisingly well-educated. But there was something about him, something different from any man she'd met before.

Oh, she knew without a doubt she was an enormous thorn in his side, but he managed to remain civil. A rather colossal feat in her mind. Few men ever condoned her doing books, and she often had to say when handing them over, that she was simply running the errands for her father, when in reality she'd done all the work. She could play the distasteful game when need be. But she didn't think she'd have to play any games with Mr. Coltrane.

He crossed the room to the bookcase and pulled out more books. She recognized what they were immediately and was frankly a bit relieved. She hoped the mess that he'd first presented her with were not the actual books. And yet this next stack looked older, more tattered than the last.

"Make yourself comfortable, Mrs. Baker. This isn't going to be an easy task."

He piled the books in front of her on the desk, then moved back to his chair. "These are the books I—we inherited from old man Cofield, who most definitely was no bookkeeper. And his handwriting was basically a scrawl."

"Ah, I see. So the others are your attempts to correct them?"

He nodded. "And you're right. I'm no bookkeeper."

"Well. Not to worry. I have seen some poor books in my day." She stood and removed her hat, then began unbuttoning her coat. "By the way, who is Canna?"

She did her best to ignore how he stared at her as she removed her jacket. She had to be comfortable, and sitting at a desk perusing numbers and such for potentially hours was extremely unpleasant all buttoned up. Men were such ninnies. It wasn't as if she were stripping down to her drawers.

Heat crept up her throat at the thought and how it easily led her to ideas she'd not considered since before she was married. Averting her gaze, she moved to hang her things on a peg.

"Hmm?"

She turned by the door at his reply to find him looking at her in the oddest way. His elbows rested on the arms of his chair and his fingers were steepled against his mouth where he partially hid a small crooked grin. The look was incredibly unnerving, but she had to dismiss it, because it was making her far warmer than was safe, not to mention reviving her previous thoughts.

But becoming overheated was dangerous to her health. It was a sign, a trigger of a seizure to come, and she couldn't afford to have one, not here, not now.

She'd had a lengthy letter exchange with the local doctor, grateful he was a forward thinking man and not prone to the myths and stigmatisms associated with epilepsy, and he was fully prepared to administer her care. But to have a seizure here in front of Mr. Coltrane would destroy the progress she'd made, and only be a source of proof that she was unfit to own or run a business. To some she did not even have the right to exist.

Forcing that thought from her mind, she returned to her chair and retrieved her reticule, making certain her bromide vile was inside. With a breath of relief, she set her bag aside and prepared for actual work. The puzzle of numbers would calm her and when the coffee arrived, she could slip a drop into her cup.

She lifted the oldest looking journal from the stack, determined not to look at Mr. Coltrane unless absolutely necessary. "You called out to someone named Canna. I assume that is the young man I saw earlier sweeping the floor."

"Ah, yes. Canna is—Canna is a kid that helps out around here."

She flipped to the first page and was dismayed at the sight of the original ledger. "I see. And do you—we pay this Canna?"

"A place to sleep and food. If you can get the kid to take it, that is."

She lifted her head from the scratchings in the book. "The child won't eat?"

That crooked grin she'd spied earlier returned, dimpling his cheek.

Blood rushed to her face, but she refrained from fanning herself. This would not do. She could not get overheated. Although, she had to admit the heat she was feeling wasn't what she normally felt before a seizure. As a matter of fact, she could only recall one other time she felt this way around a man. And that man was her husband.

She'd practically swooned when he'd first come to call on her, and nearly every day after that. It was upon her wedding night that she learned he was not what he seemed. From that moment on, she felt nothing but revulsion when she was around him.

"Canna is an orphan and incredibly proud," Mr. Coltrane said, pulling her from her thoughts.

He sat back in his chair with a shake of his head. "Refuses to take any kind of charity, will argue you to death on it. I can't begin to tell you how hard it was to get the kid to sleep on an old cot in the kitchen, instead of up in a hay loft over at the livery stable. Wouldn't take the extra room upstairs. Said it wasn't honest, said something as special as a proper bedroom had to be earned. So I hired the kid. But even then the kid wouldn't sleep in the room."

He's not only handsome, he's incredibly kind, she thought.

Clearing the tightness from her throat, she returned her gaze to the book in her hand. "So he fetches and carries, makes coffee, and sweeps?"

"Yes, sweeping is something the kid does constantly."

The door opened and in came the topic of their discussion. He looked much like the street urchins she'd seen in New York. But then without a mother to make him wash his face and hands, come his hair, and tidy his clothes, it was no wonder he looked to be such a rag-a-muffin.

The young boy placed the tray on the side of Mr. Coltrane's desk while sneaking veiled looks at Hattie. A hat covered the child's head, and scraggly long hair hid his eyes well. Hattie had the feeling it was planned that way. But then there was no telling what sort of life the boy had before being taken in by Mr. Coltrane. Although a saloon wasn't at all appropriate for raising a child, it was better than sleeping in a hay loft.

"Thanks Canna. That's all for now."

"Sure thing, Colt. Just give a yell if you need anything."

The boy slipped away as Mr. Coltrane lifted her cup, and said, "I hope you like it black. I have sugar, but can't stand the taste of milk."

"I do take a lump of sugar in my coffee, but I'm not overly fond of milk either."

He dropped the lump into her cup and handed it to her with a spoon to stir. Surprised by his proper manners, she'd bet her best hat that he'd been raised by someone from the upper classes. Or he knew how to behave in almost any situation so that he could better win his competitors' money. Either way, she was quite glad that he was so polite.

She placed the cup to her lips just as he said, "Oh, I must warn you about Canna's coffee."

Hattie's eyes flew wide open as she forced the bitter brew down her throat.

Mr. Coltrane chuckled with a small smile of chagrin. "I'm sorry I wasn't fast enough."

"I think I may need to give Canna a few lessons on how to make coffee." She set the cup aside, then glanced at him as he took a sip. "That is unless you like it this way."

He grimaced and shook his head. "Can't stand it, but I need coffee and I need to keep the kid occupied."

She smiled wide, unable to retain it any longer. "You, Mr. Coltrane, are the first true gentleman I've met in a very long time."

He laughed and set his cup down. "Don't let it get around. I have a reputation to maintain as a cutthroat gambler. It would kill business if everyone thought I was a sucker for a pretty face or orphan kids."

"I wouldn't be surprised if they saw through your charade already. But I promise to keep mum about it."

After an hour of quietly going over the books, their conversations about business and nothing more, Hattie stood and stretched the kinks out of her back while Mr. Coltrane lit a cheroot.

"Oh, I'm sorry. You don't mind do you, Mrs. Baker?"

"No, not at all. And please, call me Hattie. It seems reasonable since we're partners for the time being."

"I agree, and call me Colt."

She walked around the office, touching the few novels on the shelf, and the several legal tomes. "You have very interesting reading selections here." She wandered the cozy office, ran her hand along the arm of a leather sofa in the corner, and admired how neat and tidy the room was. "This room reminds me of my father's office in New York."

"You said he was a business man and a banker. May I ask his name?"

She gave him a sheepish grin. "Bertram Little. Not famous, but a good solid businessman who did very well for himself and for his family."

"Did he not provide for you? I realize you were married, but you are a widow and one would think a father…"

"He did provide for me, but not in the conventional way. I have enough to live comfortably for the rest of my life."

She clasped her hands in front of her at the stretch of the truth. To be honest with anyone other than herself about her true financial status would not be wise. She'd learned that a long time ago. In truth she was actually a woman of means, a rather wealthy woman of means. But she'd always been frugal and disliked the high society passions. It was such a waste, when so many were without. The lawyers who managed the trust her father had created for her couldn't understand her, but they sent her what she requested. Just enough to be comfortable. And she wanted to feel she'd earned the money, not just inherited it.

She looked at Colt across the room where he leaned against the large oak desk studying her, and smiled.

"I know. I'm a puzzle. You aren't the first to think it. But I don't want to be just comfortable," she confessed. "I know for some it is incomprehensible, but I'd be unhappy if I were just—taken care of."

He chuckled. "I suspect you could take that comfortable living wherever you like, but you want to make your own mark on the world."

"Yes, exactly! I'm so glad you understand. It makes our working together so much more pleasant."

"Yes it does. Although doing it here, in the backrooms of a dusty old saloon is a bit much." He motioned around the room, then held up his hand before she could respond. "I know you had other plans for the place. But you're willing to work with what you've got."

"Yes, and it isn't as awful as you make it sound. It's just—different."

He straightened, put out his cheroot, and rubbed the back of his neck. "So, about working with what you've got, have you had enough of the books for one day?"

"Oh, but they're still several more journals to go through."

"Hattie, you don't have to do it all in one day. Staring at those scrawls all day is bound to give even someone with your obvious expertise in accounting a headache."

She let out a soft laugh. "I can now see why you had such trouble with them. Mr. Cofield's hand was dreadful."

"And yet you've managed to figure out most of what I'd given up on long ago. But they're not going anywhere and I'm getting hungry for some lunch. Why don't I show you around the rest of the saloon and we'll send Canna to get us some sandwiches from the hotel."

"I think that's a grand idea. I did want a look at the storeroom."

He nodded and escorted her out the door into the small hallway.

"The store room is right down here."

A quick perusal of the room was all she needed for the moment. Noting the overall condition of the place, other than what she'd spied when she'd first peeked inside, was enough. She'd take a proper inventory another day.

Colt motioned down the hall toward a door. "There's a back set of stairs to the rooms above, and at the other end of the hall is a kitchen."

"What's that door at the end of the hall beyond the kitchen? Is it to the outside?"

"No that's to the business next door, which is empty right now. The kitchen has a back door—the only back door out. But I keep that locked and so should you. We don't want anyone sneaking in back here.

"Oh no, they'd have access to the office and the supplies. Definitely not."

"I was thinking more of not getting shot in the back, but those are good reasons too," he said with a chuckle.

She jerked to a halt and grasped his arm at her elbow. "Colt, you can't mean to say…"

"This is a saloon and it can get pretty rough."

"But…"

He gave her a crooked grin and clasped her hands where they clutched his arm. His dark brown eyes, almost black in the dim light of the hallway looked down at her with, dare she think it, desire? Would he kiss her? If he did, it would be a complete and utter disaster. She could not get involved with the man. But she couldn't deny how much she wished he would kiss her, although they were virtually strangers.

"It's alright. Don't worry too much about it. I do my best to not take a man's last dollar or the family farm."

She forced herself to blink away thoughts of kisses and caresses, things she'd never truly experienced, and focused on what he was saying. "But you won the saloon from Mr. Cofield."

"I did, but the old man was glad of it. He was ready to move on." He chuckled, breaking the spell she felt weaving around her. "You need to have faith in me. I can read people pretty well."

With that, he took her by the elbow and lead her back into the saloon.

"Hanson, Canna, Mrs. Baker is, as of now, half owner of this establishment."

Canna let out a guffaw, then quickly cut it off as the kid realized he was serious.

"Hattie, this is George Hanson, whom you've already met. If anyone knows anything about bartending, it's George."

"It's a pleasure to meet you."

He silently placed the glass he was wiping down and took her offered hand into his massive paw, and ever so slightly bowed over it. "Ma'am."

Another gentleman? What was it about this place that seemed to breed men of this sort? Even the sheriff, although a tad rough around the edges, had been more than cordial.

"Hanson isn't much of a talker, but if you ever have a question or need anything and I'm not available, you go to him."

He turned to Canna, who was sitting with eyes wide open in shock. "Canna, run over to the hotel and get us a couple of sandwiches."

Canna hopped down off the stool and took the money from Colt's hand. There was something not quite right about the child, Hattie realized.

"Um, you want the regular or something different?" Canna asked, the child's gaze no longer hidden, but raking over Hattie from her button shoes to her cameo brooch at her collar.

"The usual will be fine," Colt said.

As Canna turned to leave with a nod, the way the child moved, the mannerisms almost forced, Hattie had an epiphany. Canna was a she, not a he. But that didn't explain the girl's need to earn every scrap, to not take charity.

There was so much more going on here than Hattie could fathom in a few moments.

The child pushed backward through the swinging

door with one last glance at Hattie, then was gone.

Turning to Colt, Hattie said, "You didn't tell me Canna was a girl."

Mr. Hanson nearly dropped the glass he was cleaning, while Colt grinned and gave her a look.

"What?" she asked. "It isn't like you didn't know. I can see it in your eyes."

He chuckled. "Hattie, I can see you're going to surprise me at every turn. Yeah, Hanson and I know, but no one else does, so keep it to yourself."

"I don't understand. What do you mean no one knows? How can they not know?"

"It's safer this way."

"Safer."

"Come on, let me show you the rest of the saloon and I'll try and explain it."

They slowly climbed the stairs to the upper floor, his hand at her elbow, warming her in more ways than was proper once again. She really was going to have to come to grips with her attraction to the man.

"Canna was here for a few years before I arrived. From what I can tell, she's always acted like a boy. I think she's afraid the do-gooders will snatch her up and send her to an orphanage or something if they knew she was a girl. But even if they didn't, it's safer for her this way."

"You mean it keeps her hidden, in a way, from unscrupulous men."

He nodded. "When I realized she wasn't a boy, I did all the bluffing I could to get her to at least sleep in the kitchen. Once I got that far about two months ago, I've been struggling with how to get her to the next step. She needs a woman to show her the ropes. Lila and Patty are nice, but not quite the female influence she needs."

"Do they know about her?"

"I'm not sure. And to be honest, I don't know who does and doesn't know. It's like everyone is afraid to say anything in case the other doesn't know."

They reached the top of the landing then started down the hall.

"We'll keep an eye on her together, and I'll see what I can do to help. Do you have any idea how old she is?" Hattie asked.

"No, I don't, which has been my greatest worry. If she has a female growth spurt, there won't be hiding what she is in those clothes."

"True, but she could just be very slim, like me. Which wouldn't be all that difficult to hide."

He paused in mid-stride, bringing them to a halt, and looked her over, upsetting her nerves to no end. It was almost primal.

"Hattie, no one would ever be fooled by you dressed as a boy. You're too damn pretty, for one, and your figure—well, I'll be a gentleman and leave it at that."

"Oh, um, thank you."

He gave her a subtle wink and they continued down the hall.

"Well then, we will have to, um, determine her age, and then decide what to do if she wishes to be a girl."

"Exactly. Now you see my problem."

He motioned to the first two doors, one on each side of the hall.

"Lila and Patty are probably still asleep. I'll introduce you to them later, but these are their rooms. The empty one is at the end of the hall on the left, but Canna keeps it clean in case it's ever needed, and Hanson is here next to Lila on the right. Then I'm on the end."

Through that door at the end is the back staircase you saw downstairs beside the store room. I keep it locked, but I'll get you a key in case you need to come up here for something. I don't want you to travel through the saloon during regular hours. But keep it locked at all times."

"Ah, for similar reasons as the back door."

He nodded, then opened the door to the empty room and she peered inside. "This is actually quite nice. If I thought I could get away with it, I'd stay here instead of at the hotel."

Colt chuckled. "The town gossip would crucify you. But it isn't going to look all that great with you coming over her every day."

"Yes, I'm aware of that, but I've made my decision and refuse to let small minds dictate my life."

"Got your lunch!" Canna shouted from below.

They made their way back to the bar where Canna had placed the food.

Hattie took one of the smaller sandwiches, then looked to Canna. "Thank you for getting us lunch."

She placed a sandwich in front of the girl, who started to shake her head. "Oh, you're going to need this, dear. I have a lot of work to do, and I'm going to need you to help me."

Canna looked to Colt. "Do as she says, kid. And believe me, she isn't kidding about the work," he said.

The young girl took the offered meal, but with obvious hesitation. "What kind of work?"

"I want to do a full cataloging of the store room, including what is behind the bar, although I can already see that Mr. Hanson keeps it incredibly organized. So that portion won't take long."

"Don't sound like too much work," Canna said, around a mouthful of bread and cheese.

"True, but I can think of several other things I need help with. I'd like very much to polish this brass footrest and wax the bar and the banister. And the coffee you made. Although it was—nice, I like to have mine a special way. Would you like me to show you? Or I could just make my own and you won't have to worry about it. But you can decide on that later. And I suspect the kitchen might need cleaning and putting to rights."

"The kitchen is clean," Canna said, then snuck a napkin to her lips. Hattie realized that the girl was watching and mimicking her every move, which was a very good sign. She wanted to be a lady.

"I'm glad to hear it, but my guess would be that it's empty of anything other than coffee and sugar."

"Afraid so," Colt said. "None of us are all that good with cooking. Beans maybe, but nothing as good as what we can get from the hotel restaurant."

"Well then, I think cooking will be one of my tasks as well. This sandwich is nice, but, well, I do prefer my own cooking."

Colt's sandwich stopped midway to his mouth. "You cook?"

She grinned. "Yes, I do. As a matter of fact, that was my plan for the saloon. I was going to turn it into an upscale restaurant."

Colt's chuckle started low and ran on for quite a few seconds before fading.

She dropped the remains of her sandwich, one she wasn't enjoying in the least to the bar. "I don't think it's funny," she said, a firm frown on her face.

He reigned in his joviality and grinned at her. "I'm sorry, I'm not laughing at your idea. After learning something about your background, I assumed you had servants. As a matter of fact, I can't recall ever knowing a debutante who could cook, clean, and do books."

Hattie cocked her head at him and his telling words. A debutante? Where would he have ever met a debutante, unless of course her suspicions about him were true? He was so much more than a gentleman gambler. She'd had vast experience in dealing with the lower classes through her father's philanthropist efforts, and this man was no average gambler.

Her scowl disappeared, and she said, "A debutante that always had a difficult time staying idle. But I do enjoy a challenge, especially in the kitchen."

"I have no doubt of that. But I'm not sure a swanky restaurant would do all that well here. Although we're growing rapidly, this is still cattle and farm country. Not all that many upper-class types that would want to experience fine dining."

"Yes, I'd considered that in my research, but needed to be here to see and examine the prospect first hand. I can see now, however, that my initial idea would need a some adjusting. But I think the food itself would've been a much-needed improvement over this," she said, waving a hand over the remains of her lunch.

"I know I can speak for all of us, that we'd like nothing more than better meals. But I don't want you to feel obligated—"

"Don't be silly. I have to eat too, and it's much easier to cook for several than it is for one."

A shout was heard from the balcony. "Hey Canna, how about some coffee up here?"

Hattie looked to the ladies on the upper level and was relieved to see that they wore somewhat suitable clothing, although a bit tattered. She wasn't sure if they'd appear in their undergarments or not.

Canna hopped off the stool and started to the back door toward the kitchen. "Coming!"

Hattie called to the young girl. "Canna, when you've made your delivery, will you bring me a pad and pencil from the office? I'd like us to start on the inventory immediately before shopping for kitchen supplies."

She nodded, then disappeared to do the saloon girls bidding.

"We've got thirty-two shot glasses," Mr. Hanson murmured.

Hattie paused in sliding off the stool and gave Colt a glance.

He grinned back at her and shrugged his shoulders. "He manages the bar, tells me what to order and when."

"Interesting. Very well." She moved to the opening at the end of the bar and took a quick visual inspection. "It's neat, clean, and well organized. You are to be commended, Mr. Hanson. But I will still need to put the details on paper."

The quiet man nodded as he continued to dry another glass. Canna arrived with a pad and paper after delivering the coffee.

"Thank you, Canna," Hattie said.

While cleaning up their lunch wrappings, Canna said, "Colt, Lila and Patty want to talk to you."

He gave a nod, but made no move to hurry and see what it was they wanted. Hattie was glad of that. She wanted to prove to him that she was more than capable of running the saloon. Even if it was only from behind a set of books. She would never consider socializing with the customers, as she had no doubt that Colt did so every evening.

Hattie placed the pad on the counter and looked to Mr. Hanson. "Now, you say there are thirty-two shot glasses. Is that behind the bar alone or are there more in the store room?"

"A case of two dozen in the store room. Thirty-two here. Forty beer mugs here, another case of thirty in the store room. Fifteen tumblers here, a case of a dozen in the store room…"

The stoic bartender continued itemizing everything behind the bar and what was in the store room. Hattie was stunned to find she had difficulty keeping up, but managed to get it all on paper. She knew in her heart that there was no need to double check his counts.

She'd met men like him before through her father. They could calculate large amounts in their head and retain a vast number of details. Those men saw her as nothing but a secretary taking dictation, and for the most part that is what she was. But in this case, it was her saloon…well their saloon and she needed all the information in a proper format so that she could manage things appropriately. She could do sums in her head, but she found that having it all written down in neat columns made life so much simpler when trying to determine profit and loss.

"Well, Mr. Hanson, that's quite a lot of information, and I do not doubt for one moment it's accuracy. Thank you very much. You have saved Canna and I a great deal of time."

"You're welcome, ma'am."

"Well, that leaves us with the kitchen." She looked

at Canna, who continued watching her every move from beneath her scraggily hair. "I'll go and fetch my things from the office, then we'll meet in the kitchen. I'd like to see what there is to work with before purchasing a lot of supplies."

Colt slid off his stool and escorted her to the back door toward the office. Once they entered the hallway, he said, "You don't have to cook for us, Hattie. I think you have enough to do with the books."

She entered the office and put the pad and paper with the inventory beside the books still laid out on the edge of the desk. "I know I don't, but I really do like to cook and I'd much rather not waste money on food such as our lunch."

Colt took her coat from the peg on the wall and held it out for her to slip into. "You didn't like your sandwich all that much, did you? You barely took two bites."

"Although it was edible it was lacking anything worthy of noting. It was something to simply fill an empty stomach. Not the kind of cooking I prefer."

"I can't argue with that, but I think I'll be getting the lion's share out of this forced partnership."

She slid into the coat, then his hands rested on her shoulders, causing her to pause. His lips were far too close to her ear, she could feel his warm breath upon her neck.

"And I'm going to relish every moment of it," he murmured, sending shivers down her spine. The kind of shivers that made a woman want things she shouldn't want.

She cleared her throat and stepped from his grasp. "Well, we'll see how you like my cooking." She moved to the small mirror and concentrated on placing her hat on her head, ignoring his reflection, refusing to look into those dark eyes. "You may decide that I'm no better than the hotel's cook."

He moved to behind the desk and opened a drawer. "I seriously doubt that." He retrieved a satchel and pulled out several dollar bills. "But here," he said, handing them to her from across the desk. "Buy whatever it is you want from Jenkins General Store. Right next door to it, is the butcher."

"I have plenty of money—"

"You're planning on feeding all of us, right? Then the saloon should pay."

"Well, yes, you're right it should. Thank you." She took the bills and headed toward the door.

"And anything you and Canna can't carry back, just have them deliver it."

"I'm sure we can manage. I wish to start with a small amount to be sure we're all happy with my selections." She paused in the doorway. "I meant to ask. Is there possibly a root cellar of some sort? I know it would be uncommon for a business, but—"

"Yes, there is, and there's water too. The kitchen is actually fairly modern. Cofield liked gadgets and new inventions. But Canna will show you everything."

"Well, thank you again. This has been a very interesting day."

He chuckled and moved to the doorway and took her hand. "I couldn't agree more." He kissed the back of her hand, which had her stuck in a tiny breath. He turned her hand over and slipped two keys into the palm and closed her fingers around them. "These are the keys to the back door in the kitchen and the back stairs."

"Thank you. And not to worry, I don't wish to go

through the saloon. I can only imagine the affect that would have on the festivities," she said with a small giggle.

"True, and it's safer this way and much simpler for you and Canna." He let go of her hand and followed her through the door, closing it behind him. "And don't let Canna convince you she's allowed in the saloon during regular hours. She tries to slip through from time to time. Curious I suppose, but it's off limits."

With a nod, she turned and continued down the hall to the kitchen, all the while pretending the touch of his lips to her hand meant nothing to her. That she felt no silent thrill. It would not do to become infatuated with the man—if she wasn't already.

****

Hattie noticed Canna eyeing the bits of ribbon and lace in the general store and had a feeling that changing the caterpillar into a butterfly wouldn't be all that difficult. The hard part was going to be convincing the girl, and then there was the problem with her sleeping arrangements.

She had hopes she could convince her to stay with her at the hotel, but that was a separate battle.

Turning her attention to her list and all the work she still needed to accomplish that afternoon, she approached the store keeper.

"Good afternoon. I'd like to purchase several items to stock an empty kitchen."

"An empty kitchen, you say? What kitchen would that be?"

The man was a bit gruff and downright rude, not to mention he smelled. She didn't think he had any idea what a bar of soap even looked like, but Hattie needed the supplies. "The Golden Lady Saloon's kitchen. I only wish to have enough for a few days. Enough for Canna and myself to carry."

"So, Colt's got a new woman, eh? Patty and Lila can't like that much," he said with a snide chuckle.

Canna's eyes widened, while Hattie's hackles were raised. She knew this would be a trial, but there was no avoiding it. She may as well begin here.

"Mr. Jenkins, there are two things I abhor, ill manners and inaccurate information. Therefore, to be clear on the matter, although it is none of your business whatsoever, I am no one's *woman.* I own half interest in the Golden Lady, left to me by my dead husband, and plan to operate as bookkeeper and cook for the moment. Nothing more.

Now I would appreciate it if you would kindly keep your sordid thoughts to yourself and fill this order so that I might prepare an evening meal for Mr. Coltrane and the others."

"Um, yes, ma'am." The scowl deepened on his face as he took the list from her gloved hand, muttering beneath his breath.

As he filled a box and laid various things on the counter, Hattie looked about the store for anything else she might have forgotten and caught sight of Canna gently fingering that bolt of calico on the end of the counter.

"Keep your dirty paws off that fabric!" Jenkins shouted.

Canna scuttled away like a terrified rabbit, while Hattie had to bight her tongue. She didn't like the odious man in the least, but skinning him verbally yet again could cause him to deny her service, and he was the only general store in town.

A few moments later, he stacked the items into a box and gave her the total. She quickly paid him in cash, then moved to pick up the box, but Canna shoved her aside to do the job.

"Thank you, Canna, that's very nice of you."

As they left the store, Hattie came to a stop at the door and turned to look at the horrible man.

"If you wish for me to purchase from your store again, Mr. Jenkins, I suggest you improve your behavior, which has been abominable."

"Ain't no other store," he replied with a slimy grin.

"All of the items I will need in the future can easily be had from New York. And to be perfectly clear, I have no qualms whatsoever of ordering them. Therefore, I suggest you work on your customer service, or lack thereof, before you lose a great deal of business. Good-day, Mr. Jenkins."

Canna's mouth remained agape as Hattie passed her by the door, and she cast the young girl a wink. The child quickly fell in step beside her along the boardwalk. Hattie knew she had something to say, but she didn't make a sound. She wondered if it had more to do with trying to remain invisible in town and not draw attention to herself, rather than any type of repercussions from what she wanted to say.

Thankfully, they didn't have the same issue with the butcher. He seemed happy with the large order Hattie made and promised to have someone deliver more of the same the following day.

On their way back to the saloon, both their arms laden with boxes and packages, Canna seemed unable to remain silent any longer.

"Jenkins is an ass to everyone, but I sure like how you skewered him."

"He is a rather horrible man. He feels safe to say whatever he wants, behave as badly as he likes because he holds most of the town in the palm of his hand owning the only general store."

"You really going to do your own ordering? Ain't that expensive?"

"You mean, isn't that expensive. And yes, I plan to do my own ordering for some of the items I like in a kitchen. Mr. Jenkins didn't have the quality I prefer. But to answer your other question, no it's not more expensive, if done properly. Actually, it will be cheaper and much more efficient. However, I needed these things today and ordering can take weeks, so we had no choice but to purchase them from the general store."

Hattie led the way to the back of the saloon and the kitchen door, then paused. "Canna, if you ever go in there again, for whatever reason, please do not go alone. I suspect that Mr. Jenkins will take my words out on you, and I can't have that on my conscience. I wouldn't want anything to happen to you, especially because of something I said or did. Do you understand?"

Canna grinned. "I only been in there a few times cause he don't like me there no how. So, you don't have to worry about me, Mrs. Baker."

With a smile, she replied, "Call me Hattie."

Both wearing wide grins, they went inside and piled their purchases on the large center table. Hattie took off her hat and coat and let out a deep breath as she sank into a chair. She was overdoing it, she knew it, she could feel it. A seizure was near at hand, but she'd been so excited she'd forgotten to stop and take a rest. That was the only way she'd managed to keep them at bay. A small rest every day after lunch worked well, but today she'd not stopped for more than a few minutes and the sandwich at lunch had been so abysmal she barely ate. Another thing she was not supposed to do, go without a decent meal.

As if a clock had struck the hour, her hands began to quiver in her lap and her head grew fuzzy. She needed her medicine, although at this late stage it did little to stop the seizure, but it could keep it from becoming a horrible writhing, twisting nightmare. She'd not had a seizure like that since before she met her husband.

"Canna, would you fetch me a glass of water please?" she asked, as she fumbled with her reticule for the small vile.

Canna appeared beside her with a glass and a concerned frown on her dirt-smudged face. "You okay?"

"No, I'm not, to be honest. Help me put a drop of this in the water, and make sure I drink it, please."

"Um sure, okay."

A few moments passed and Hattie could feel the water sliding down her throat. A few moments more or perhaps it had been several minutes, she couldn't be sure, the fuzziness began to fade and she knew she was still sitting in the chair, not writhing around on the floor like a lunatic. She'd been lucky. The spell was a small one after all, but she could never be certain. A grand mal seizure was always a possibility.

She opened her eyes to find Canna kneeling on the floor beside her, holding her hand, and watching her every move.

With a small smile, she patted the back of the child's hand. "I'm alright now."

"You sure you're okay? You looked a million miles

away and you shook all over. I was afraid you'd topple right out of the chair."

"I'm sorry I frightened you, dear. I just overdid it today. The doctor insists I rest every afternoon, but there is so much work to be done, and I suppose I was excited about cooking for all of you, that I let the time get away from me. But I'm fine now. I just have to pay better attention."

"I'll remind you when you need to rest. I won't let you work yourself sick. I promise."

"Thank you, Canna. It's nice to have someone to help me behave," she said with a small smile.

"You need more of this?" she asked, holding up the glass.

"No, pour that down the drain, please. It's not something I should take too often."

She moved to the sink and did as she was told. "What is it? Laudanum?"

"No, it's a bromide, but it can be as addictive as Laudanum, so I have to be very careful with it. But Canna, I need you to keep this to yourself. It's not something that people understand. And, if you would, help me should I need it?"

With a wide smile, Canna returned to her side. "Sure you can. I promise not tell another soul, and to fetch your medicine or even the doctor if it looks bad."

Hattie reached out and tucked a stray greasy strand of hair behind the child's ear. "Thank you, Canna. I couldn't have a better friend."

Chapter Three

Early that evening Colt followed his nose down the hall toward the kitchen, unable to ignore the delicious smells wafting through the building. Whatever Hattie was preparing for their dinner made his stomach rumble. If she was as good a cook as she was bookkeeper, they were in for a treat. This could actually be the best deal he'd ever made.

Upon entering the kitchen, he found Hattie and Canna with their heads bent over a piece of paper.

"Looks like more than cooking is going on in here."

Hattie smiled, and Colt took pause, then shook it off as quickly as the sensation came. The best deal he ever made did have its problems, namely, attraction.

"It's more of a slight reading lesson on how I prepare coffee," Hattie said.

"Ah, I see. Canna, I'm sorry I never thought to ask if you wanted to learn how to read."

"I know some of it, it's just been a long while."

"Have you ever been in a schoolroom?" he asked.

"Not really, more or less outside, below the window when it wasn't too cold."

A look passed over Hattie's face then she quickly covered it with a small smile. "Well now you can learn as much as you want whenever you like." She gave a slight nod in Colt's direction, and he gave one in return.

"Hanson was wondering about the smells coming

from in here," Colt said. He stuck his nose over an open pot and his mouth watered.

Hattie grinned. "Just Mr. Hanson?"

"Oh, well Lila and Patty too."

"Uh-huh."

He laughed with a shrug. "Okay, we all wanted to know. Looks and smells like stew."

"Yes, it's stew and it's ready. But it occurred to me that dinner time is going to be different for all of you. I intend on keeping with a normal schedule for myself. I have never been a late-night person and don't intend to change."

"If the stew is as good as it smells, we'll be happy with whatever and whenever you wish to cook."

"I usually get Colt coffee around ten. Hanson's not a coffee drinker," Canna said.

"And Patty and Lila?"

Canna shrugged. "I fetch for them when they ask. They don't have a schedule."

"Hattie, cook when you want to. We'll all adjust and be very grateful."

With a soft blush, she ladled out stew into a bowl for him. "Sit and eat, so you can win all your poker games on a full stomach."

He chuckled and did as he was told.

Colt lifted his spoon with a nod to Canna. "Canna, why don't you take one to Hanson, but mind you stay in the doorway."

"Sure thing, Colt."

With lightning speed, the child had a bowl of stew in hand and was gone before Hattie could turn around.

"My goodness," she said.

"I told you. She's determined to earn her keep." Colt

dipped his spoon into the thick mouthwatering concoction, blew across it to cool, then placed it in his mouth. He fell still and let his lids slide closed as he savored the best stew he'd had in years.

"Good?" Hattie asked, as she sat across from him.

"You've no idea." With that he continued his meal in silence and a look of glee on his face.

Canna returned and said the girls wanted a taste too.

"Of course, dear. Make up two bowls and take them up the back stairs to their rooms," Hattie said, handing Canna the key. She could have filled the bowls herself, but she was relishing watching Colt lap up every drop in his bowl. There was something in seeing that kind of enjoyment on a man's face.

Or maybe it was just this man.

"May I please have a little more?" he asked, his mouth tipped up at the corner, setting Hattie's heart to flutter, if only for a moment.

"Of course." She'd known the man for less than a day and yet felt as if she'd known him for ages. But the battle with her attraction to him was beyond distracting. She would have to work harder to keep her sensibilities about her, since it appeared they would be in close company often.

She ladled more stew into his bowl as the bar noise grew louder.

"Sounds like it's kicking up out there," Canna said, returning from her delivery.

"Looks like a good crowd tonight," Colt said.

Canna took a seat at the table, her bowl so much smaller than the others, but at least she was eating.

Colt sat back from the table. "I can't thank you enough for that dinner, Hattie."

"Canna helped."

Hattie took his bowl and placed it in the sink. "After I clean up the kitchen, I'll be heading back to the hotel. I want to leave before it gets dark."

"I'll escort you back," Colt said, rising from his chair.

She looked at him over her shoulder from where she stood by the sink. "That's very kind of you, but not necessary. I'm sure I'll be fine."

He let out a heavy sigh. "I suppose it wouldn't look all that good for me to escort you anyway."

She quickly dried her hands and moved to stand before him. "I'd be honored for you to escort me, Colt. I just didn't think it was needed."

That crooked grin of his warmed her insides.

"A lady should always be escorted. I'll go check on things in the saloon, then be back here in fifteen minutes."

She smiled. "In that case, thank you. I'll be ready."

****

The following morning, after having tossed and turned most of the night, her thoughts on Colt, Hattie awoke tired but with a bit of blush in her cheeks. He was such a wonderful man, and she didn't care one bit what the hotel manager thought. Colt had left her at the door of the hotel and tipped his hat to her. He didn't kiss her, or her hand. He was the perfect gentleman, if the towns' people couldn't see what he really was, then they were all blind as the proverbial bat.

Hattie made her way along the boardwalk then turned down the small side street to the back of the saloon and the kitchen door. She unlocked the door, and remembered to lock it behind her after she entered, then fell absolutely still.

The sight of Canna asleep on the small cot in the corner made her heart twist. She'd never know what it was to have a child of her own. She'd had hopes when she'd married, but they were quickly dashed when John revealed his true colors. They'd consummated their vows, but it had been horrible. A quick tossing up of her nightgown and the deed was done. And too, she worried about her illness and having to tend to a baby.

She shivered at the unwelcome memory and horrible imaginings and focused on preparing a hearty breakfast, and went straight to work. There were men to be fed as well as a child, and possibly a pair of soiled doves.

She thought of Patty and Lila as she sifted flour into a bowl. They'd been introduced, but that was about all. Although they did thank her through Canna for the stew. She supposed they were afraid of what she thought of them and their chosen careers, but with luck and time they'd see that she had nothing against them.

"Watcha' doin'?"

She smiled as Canna rubbed the sleep from her eyes. The fact she was a girl was all too prevalent in her unguarded movements. "I'm making bread, and once I get this done, I'm going to make a batch of flapjacks. Do you like flapjacks?"

She eased off her cot and pulled at her oversized clothes, making sure everything telling was hidden. "I guess. I'm not much of a breakfast person."

"That's alright, but would you give me a hand with them? I have a feeling that Colt and Mr. Hanson will want some, so I intend to make quite a stack."

Canna shrugged. "Sure. Just tell me what to do. Like with the coffee."

"Perfect. I'll be done with this in just a moment."

"I've never seen anyone make bread before. Is it hard to do?"

"No, not really. Sometimes, of course, it doesn't rise, but usually it comes out alright. Would you like to learn?"

The child shrugged again with a faint nod, but Hattie could see the keen interest in her eyes.

"Why don't you start the coffee while I finish this up? Then we'll get that stack of flapjacks going while the bread rises."

"Sure!" With a bright smile, Canna snatched the coffee pot and the directions and went to work, making sure she followed every step with care.

Hattie knew she was a very bright child, and was eager to see how far and how fast she would grow, both in mind and in appearance. She'd already stopped hiding her eyes behind her hair in Hattie's presence, and with luck and perhaps some much needed love, she would grow to be a very capable young woman.

After Canna finished making the coffee and the first round of flapjacks, Hattie managed to convince Canna to at least taste the very thing she helped prepare.

"After all, we both need to eat a good meal. We have a lot of work to do today," she said to the child.

Hattie set two plates on the table with a lady-size number of flapjacks, and a jar of maple syrup. Canna watched then copied every move Hattie made, from pouring a small amount over her serving to how she held her silverware.

"Good?" Hattie asked, seeing that Canna had eaten half her plate in record time.

The girl nodded with a grin. "I can't believe I helped

make this."

"And let's not forget the coffee and the stew last night. You're very good in the kitchen, Canna. I for one, appreciate your help."

With smiles on their faces, they finished their breakfast and tidied up the kitchen. Just as Canna dried the last dish, a pair of somewhat disheveled men strolled into the kitchen. It was barely nine, so they were up quite early.

"Good morning, gentlemen. Care for some breakfast? Canna has made a fabulous pot of coffee."

"Canna made it?" Colt asked.

Hattie cast a sideways wink to them. "Yes, she did. Canna would you pour Colt a cup? And what about you, Mr. Hanson? I understand you aren't a coffee drinker, but perhaps I could interest you in some tea or milk?"

He cast a sheepish glance toward Colt. "Milk please, ma'am."

Canna placed their drinks before them and fetched two clean plates, while Hattie pulled a double stack of flapjacks from the oven where she'd been keeping them warm. She'd had a feeling they would seek out the aroma of breakfast cooking. "Canna also helped with the flapjacks. Here you go, gentlemen. Eat up."

Hattie relished their hearty appetites and let them eat in peace. Canna cast her a crooked grin when they both made yummy noises as they ate.

"Well now, since you are both set for your breakfast, Canna and I are going to get started on today's list of chores. Just leave the plates and we'll get to them later."

"Hattie," Colt called, as she and Canna started through the doorway. "Thank you. Both of you."

Canna giggled, just as a young girl should, but

quickly covered her mouth and ducked down the hall. Still, it was progress.

"You're both very welcome. I will do my best to always have some breakfast either warming in the oven or atop the stove for when you wake. So, you don't need to jump out of bed half dressed, afraid it will all be gone when you arrive."

With that she smiled and strolled down the hall after Canna, a large wash pail in her hand.

"Am I dreaming?" Colt muttered.

"If you are, then so am I," Hanson replied. "Don't know how all this happened, but I am a happy man."

Colt slapped him on the back with a laugh. "That makes two of us."

With that they finished off all the flapjacks and both agreed that whatever Hattie wanted or wanted them to do, they'd do it.

****

Colt and Hanson watched, or rather, stayed out of the way, as Hattie and her new right hand scrubbed down the saloon floor then proceeded to give it a good polish. She'd cleaned all the light sconces one day, the brass railings another day, the stair rails had been waxed yet another, and now the floors. He'd never seen it look so good and yet hated it. By night time the men and their muddy boots would scuff the floor up but good, ruining all their hard work.

"There. Now that's a proper floor," Hattie said, wiping her brow with the back of her hand.

"You know how dirty it's gonna get tonight?" Canna asked.

Hattie smiled. "It isn't the beauty of it as much as it is the longevity."

"Huh?"

"By waxing the floor every so often it will lengthen its life. I know it will be filthy by morning, and I have to say you've done a fabulous job of keeping it tidy, but if we don't scrub and wax it every so often, eventually all the scuffing and scraping will eat through the floor and it will have to be repaired."

Colt glanced at Hanson and they shared a shrug. It made sense what she was saying, just not something either of them thought would actually happen. It would take more than a few years for the floor to need the kind of repair Hattie was talking about, and both men knew that there was a good chance the saloon would be gone by then. Probably turned into another general store or some such thing.

With Willow Bend growing the way it was, new ways of building, new types of businesses, new laws and regulations, it wouldn't be a simple town for too many more years. Especially when they became a state. But he supposed with her coming from New York, probably a large fancy house with all the polished woodwork a man could stand, the kind he remembered, she knew about taking care of what she had, and he appreciated her efforts.

"Well, gentlemen, we'll leave you to your business. We're quite done in here for today," she said, gathering their cleaning supplies and heading for the back door. "There is still a very long list of things to do in here, but they can't all be accomplished in one week. I think tomorrow Canna and I will start on the spittoons. I've been avoiding them," she said with a twinkle in her eye.

Colt watched them leave then looked back at Hanson and they shared a chuckle.

"If it makes her happy, then so be it," Colt said.

"As long as she keeps cookin', she can even clean behind the bar, if she wants," Hanson said.

Colt let out a hearty laugh, and strolled over to his favorite table, made himself comfortable and picked up a deck of cards. He enjoyed her cooking too, but if he didn't manage to stop thinking of her in other ways, he was in for some serious trouble.

The way her eyes lit up when she was excited about something, the way she wasn't afraid of anything, especially hard work, the way that one strand of hair teased the side of her neck as she bent her head while she worked on the books. He refused to think of all the bending she'd done while scrubbing. And to help him not think about it, he and Hanson had moved the tables and chairs out of their way and put them back in place as she and Canna made their way across the room. Not that they'd have allowed her and Canna to do the heavy lifting, but doing something other than watching her backside, the sway of her skirt...anything to keep his mind out of the bedroom.

He shuffled the deck, then laid out a few cards, trying to concentrate on poker and what type of game he wanted to play that night, and not the enticing woman who was his business partner.

It wasn't long before Patty and Lila appeared and a few regulars strolled in. No one was up for a game for serious money, but he played a few hands, trying not to notice the mud trail growing from the main entrance, or wince every time a chair scrapped the floor.

"Whooweee!"

Colt's head snapped up at the yell from the bar. Once again, his thoughts had been on Hattie and not on the saloon. He always watched everyone that came in, took note of each man, his mannerisms, how much money he likely had, his circumstances as a whole. And he always knew when trouble walked in. And the group of men he didn't recognize, the ones making all the racket, were definitely trouble.

"I'm out, gentlemen," he said, and threw in his cards. He rose and made his way to the end of the bar. He and Hanson exchanged glances and they knew it was going to be a rough night.

Patty sashayed over to him and slipped her arm over his shoulder. "Hey there, honey," she said, and pecked him on the cheek. She and Lila knew that if he wasn't playing cards, something was up.

With a fake grin, he leaned over and nuzzled her ear. "You and Lila slip out," he whispered. "This group doesn't look good."

"Anything you say, sugar." She cast him a wink and slipped away.

Her subtle nod aimed at Lila was all she needed to do. They both eased toward the stairs, paying attention here and there to the men along the way, but never lingering too long. They knew when Colt said get out it was for their safety.

Right before the ruckus broke out, all he could think of was how the hell he was he going to apologize to Hattie for messing up her floor.

****

After another hard day of work, and even though Canna had practically blackmailed Hattie into taking her rest in the empty room upstairs after lunch each day, she managed to get a decent night's sleep. She still dreamt of Colt every night, but the fatigue of the work they'd been doing won out each time, and now she felt refreshed and ready for another day.

With a light step she made her way down the small side-street walkway to the back door of the kitchen. She quietly unlocked the door, slipped inside and relocked it, just as she'd done every day since her arrival, hoping to not wake Canna. But when she turned, the child wasn't in her bed. There was no sign of her at all.

Assuming she'd turn up within a few minutes, she went about putting her hat and jacket on a peg, then took down the apron and tied it around her waist. After starting the coffee, she pulled out the ingredients for making a batch of biscuits, but stopped when she heard a loud thud from the hall and hurried feet.

Canna came barreling around the corner with a small basin in her hand and ran for the pump.

"What on earth?" Hattie asked.

"Can't talk, Colt needs water," she said, and frantically pumped the water.

"But—"

Before Hattie could ask another question, Canna was out the door like a shot.

Something was very wrong.

She hurried after the child as she dodged through the back door, then came to an abrupt halt at the threshold to the saloon. It looked as if a cyclone had torn through the room. Chairs upended and broken, tables on their sides, broken glassware, the mirror behind the bar smashed. Even the horrid painting had been ripped by what looks to have been a chair thrown at it.

Her gaze slid to the bar where Mr. Hanson sat on a stool, a rag against his head. He cast her a sad glance, then looked back at the wreck behind his beloved bar.

She eased into the room and found Colt sitting in a chair by a poker table in the corner with bloodied knuckles clutching a cloth. He dipped it into the basin Canna held.

"Thanks, kid," he said, then his gaze met hers. "Sorry about the floor." His swollen lip turned up a bit at the corner.

She let out a soft chuckle and shook her head. "Is everyone alright? Other than the obvious," she said, with a slight wave of her hand toward him and Mr. Hanson.

Colt nodded.

"Liar," Canna said.

"Shut up, kid."

Hattie's head snapped around. "Colt?"

"It's nothing. The kid's just overreacting."

Hattie narrowed her gaze at him, letting the matter drop for the moment and went to the bar. "Mr. Hanson, let me see that cut on your head."

"I'm alright, ma'am. I've got a hard head."

"That may be, but even a hard head can get an infection." He allowed her to examine the cut, which wasn't as deep as she feared. "Canna, go to the kitchen and in the top of the cupboard there's a bottle of camphor and some clean bandages, bring them to me please."

"Yes, ma'am."

She dabbed at Mr. Hanson's head, glad in the fact that he was sitting down. Tending his wound would likely sting a bit, but it needed to be done. "Do you have any other injuries?"

"No ma'am. Wouldn't have this one if I'd ducked sooner."

Canna returned and she quickly had Mr. Hanson bandaged. "I suggest you go to your room and rest."

"But the bar—"

"You cannot over-exert yourself. You'll only succeed in creating a bigger headache than the one you no doubt already have. Canna and I can tidy-up here."

"Do as she says, Hanson. We're not opening today anyway," Colt said.

That's when Hattie noticed his wince.

"Now it's your turn," she said, and carried her supplies to the table where he sat.

"I'm fine."

"Of course you are. That's why your knuckles are bleeding and your lip is swollen, and that looks like a lovely black eye forming. You're in perfect condition."

He started to chuckle, then stifled it as quickly as he could. "Damn."

Hattie looked to Canna. "Fetch the doctor, please Canna."

"I don't need a damn doctor. Canna! Canna!" But the child was gone.

With a painfilled grimace he rested his head back against the wall. "You are one meddling, mothering, bossy female, you know that?"

"Without a doubt." She began tending his battered hands, putting up a false front, while hoping and praying he wasn't too seriously injured.

In just a bit more than a week, the man had become important to her. She couldn't go on with the saloon without him, and she wouldn't want to. The way he grinned at her when she rattled off the list of things that needed fixing or changing, the way he watched her over his whiskey glass when she worked on the books, the sound of his voice, the scent of his cologne. And when he escorted her to her hotel, the feel of his hand over hers when she'd link her arm with his, made her feel wanted, made her feel pretty. Made her feel like a woman.

Tears were rapidly forming in her eyes and she struggled to keep them from falling.

He tipped her chin up from where she concentrated on his hands, his one eye, the only thing that seemed to have missed the beating he'd taken, gazing into hers.

"It'll be alright, Hattie. We'll clean it all up and it'll be fine."

"You idiot," she whispered, as a tear slid down her cheek. "You think the saloon is what has me upset?"

His brow furrowed. "Then what—"

"Here's the doc," Canna said, bursting into the saloon.

Hattie quickly wiped away her tears and rose to meet Dr. Farleigh. She'd managed to stop by his office on one of her errands to meet him face to face. He was an affable man, one who was always trying to stay up to date with the latest medicines and procedures.

"Mrs. Baker, it's nice to see you again," he said, removing his hat.

"It's nice to see you as well, although I dislike the circumstances."

Colt watched the interplay between them, not liking it one bit. How the hell did they know each other? Jealousy spread like green lava through is veins, and he gnashed his teeth together, then regretted it. A few had been knocked loose, as if he'd been kicked by a horse. Still, she didn't have to be all that nice to the man. They weren't in some prissy parlor.

The doctor sat down beside him, their niceties finally concluded.

"Now, what seems to be the problem, other than the

obvious abrasions?"

"I'm fine," Colt bit out, trying with all his might not to wince, but failed.

"Ah, I see." The doctor ran his hands across his ribs, then lifted his gaze to Colt's. "Not coughing blood?"

Colt shook his head.

"Then cracked most likely," the doctor said. "More than one, I'd wager."

"You'd win that bet," he replied.

"I need to bind those."

"Figured as much."

"Can you stand?"

Colt shot him a look, then nodded. He would not be carried up to bed by anyone, least of all by the handsome young doctor all the women in town, including Patty and Lila talked about. Constantly. And now Hattie was another of his followers. It made a man want to chew nails.

"Canna, make sure his bed is ready," Hattie said, then slid one of Colt's arms over her shoulder, while the bachelor doctor took him by the other.

The pain was so intense, he didn't have anything left in him to complain about the assistance. He hoped like hell he'd make it up the damn stairs without passing out.

Once on the bed, the doctor told Hattie he could manage from here. She left, but not willingly.

The doctor got off what was left of his shirt. "You'll need to stay in bed for a day or so, but not much longer after that. It's best to move around a little," the doc said, finishing up the wrapping.

"Yeah, I know. It's not the first time."

"I thought as much. If you need anything for the pain—"

"Got a bar full of pain killer, doc," he said, trying to make himself comfortable in bed, which he knew was damn near impossible.

He chuckled. "Very well. If you should need anything more, just let me know."

Colt gave a half-wave at him as he headed for the door where his mother hens were waiting and watching.

He really wished he knew why Hattie had teared up. But by the look on her face, as she stood there watching him while the doctor explained his condition, her tiny hands wringing before her, he had a feeling he was what had her upset. The pretty little lady was afraid for him.

With a satisfied grin, he fell asleep.

Chapter Four

"Canna! Coffee!" Patty yelled.

Hattie lifted her head from her task of wiping down the bar.

"Guess I'd better go?" Canna was unsure of where her duties lay.

"Yes, dear. Go run their errands for them and when you come back, we can start on the brass."

"Yes, ma'am."

Once again, the girl was off like a whirlwind, full of boundless energy Hattie envied. "Oh, to be young again and full of life," she whispered, and closed her eyes for a moment as she took a seat on a bar stool.

It had taken three days to set the saloon back to rights, but Mr. Hanson had been a great help. He'd managed to put some of the chairs back together and fixed a few table legs, while Patty and Lila did the sweeping, and helped where they could. But Hattie had relieved them all of duty the day before so they'd be ready for their reopening that night. There was only a bit of touch-up left to do.

Colt, now safely behind his desk, not over taxing his poor ribs, didn't want to keep the saloon closed for more than two nights. It just wasn't profitable, and she agreed. But there were still normal chores to tend to.

A hand fell atop hers. "Hattie?"

She blinked and looked to find Canna standing

beside her, a worried frown on her face.

"My that was fast," she said with a smile.

"They just wanted coffee. Said it was too early to eat. You okay? Do you need your medicine?"

"No, I'm alright. I suppose all the extra work is catching up with me, but I'm fine."

"I think you should rest. You can stretch out on the sofa in the office or in the empty room upstairs."

"No, no. I'm fine. Really, and there's so much more to do—"

"All the doin' can be done by me. I know what's left, so I can finish up the daily chores. Now come and lie down," she said, and helped Hattie off the stool and up the stairs.

Hattie let her escort her, as the exertion and worry over Colt, something she tried not to do, but failed, was quickly catching up with her. She didn't feel a seizure coming on, but she also knew that if she continued with her work, one was eminent.

"Canna, there's more I need to explain about my condition, but I don't want to frighten you."

She let out a sniff. "I've seen plenty of scary things. Don't worry about me."

"Well, what I have, it scares people. There could be a day when I fall to the floor and my entire body spasms out of control like a possessed demon, then I may be unconscious."

Canna squeezed her tighter by her side. "I can handle it. And if we keep you rested, it won't happen. Right?"

"That's the theory, but it could. I haven't had a seizure like that since I was fifteen. But if it should happen—"

"It won't."

She patted her hand atop her arm. "If it should, I'll need to be kept safe. Dr. Farleigh is aware of my condition, but he won't be by my side to make sure I don't harm myself. So, I'll need you to hold my arms and legs or my head so I don't bang it against something. Most that have epilepsy die from the fall or injuries during their seizure and not from the disorder itself. I know it's a lot to ask, but—"

"But it ain't gonna happen, and you need to quit worrying about it. I know what to do. I'll take care of you, I promise. Now let's get you settled."

A tear slipped from the corner of Hattie's eye. There were no words to convey her thanks nor her deep feelings for this child.

They continued down the hall, and she spied Patty and Lila lounging in one of their rooms from the corner of her eye. She knew the sight of Canna leading her like an old woman caught their attention, as their chatter ceased when they'd passed the doorway.

It felt strange to be mothered by a child this way, but she knew Canna would stand by her whenever she needed her, and she would do the same in return. She wasn't quite sure what Patty and Lila would think about all this, however. She'd made a little headway with them while they put the saloon back together, but they were still a bit skittish around her.

"Here we are. You rest up while I finish the chores," Canna said, placing her on the edge of the bed. She bent down and removed her shoes, then tucked her in.

"Thank you, Canna. I don't know what I would do without you."

"You just rest, and I'll come check on you in about

an hour."

Canna turned to the door to find Patty and Lila standing there. "Ain't nothing to see. Go back to your coffee."

"Is she sick?" Lila asked.

"No, just tired. So, leave her alone," Canna said, pushing them back through the doorway.

Hattie wanted to reply, but let her lids slid closed instead. She didn't have the strength for another long chat about her disorder, nor did she believe that Patty and Lila would understand.

"Mrs. Baker, if you need anything you just bang on that wall, and I'll come runnin'," Patty said.

"Yeah, you need anything before we start work, just let us know," Lila added.

Hattie lifted her heavy lids and smiled at the girls, all three of them. "Thank you, all of you, very much," she whispered, then fell into a sound sleep.

****

Colt entered the kitchen to find Canna slicing a large loaf of bread.

"Where's Hattie?"

"She's resting, and don't you dare disturb her," she said, waving the knife in his direction.

"Resting? Is she alright?"

"She'll be right as rain after she rests. Now, do you want one of her sandwiches or not?"

Canna's mama bear attitude had him stepping back a bit. He'd never seen her this way before. "What's got into you, kid?"

She bent her head back to the task of slicing the bread. "Nothin'. Now, do you or don't you want a sandwich? Hattie and me made up all the fixings

69

between chores."

Something was definitely not right. "Canna." He crossed to stand beside her and bent to look at her face. She was hiding something. "What's going on?"

"Nothin'. You lose your hearing or something?" She slapped the knife on the table and started to spin away, but he grabbed by the arms.

"Talk, kid, or I'll tan your hide."

She snorted, but said nothing.

"I mean it, Canna. I want answers. What—God is something wrong with Hattie? What happened? Is she sick?" He gave her a shake, determined to get her to talk.

She lifted a startled gaze to his. "Like I said, she'll be fine after she rests." She crossed her arms with a frown. "And that's all I'm saying no matter what you do to me."

Colt's heart stammered. "Where is she? In the extra room?"

Without a confirmation from the kid, he dashed down the hall and up the back stairs, ignoring the pains shooting around his ribs. He came to an abrupt stop in front of the door, suddenly lost as to how to continue.

He wasn't Hattie's keeper. Canna said she was fine. She was a grown woman, after all, who could take a rest whenever she liked. She had been working herself to the bone over the last three days, so she deserved to rest. Ladies of quality did that sort of thing, take naps and rest and such. Of course they did.

His mental reasonings didn't signal his hand to stop before it knocked on her door, however.

"Who is it?" she asked.

Colt took a long deep breath. She was fine and he'd panicked for nothing. Damn near killed himself trying to run with cracked ribs, and yet he couldn't stop the odd tattoo of his heart at the sound of her voice.

"It's Colt, I thought I'd see if you wanted to join me for lunch." He rolled his eyes at the lame excuse, but couldn't think of a better reason to be interrupting her rest.

"Um, well that's very nice, thank you, but I think I'll rest a while. You go ahead and eat. Canna knows what to do."

"Yeah, sure. Um, I'll see you later then."

"Of course, enjoy your lunch."

He opened his mouth to say something else, what, he wasn't sure, but snapped it closed before anything came out. She needed a rest, and he was keeping her from it.

He turned to go back downstairs at a much slower, healthier pace, but his way was blocked by Patty and Lila. With their arms folded in front of them and deep frowns on their faces, you'd think he'd cheated them on their paycheck or something.

"She needs to rest, not some of your fancy caller nonsense," Lila said, her lips in a firm scowl.

Patty let out a huff. "Caller, huh. He's just wonderin' what's for lunch. You can fend for yourself, Colt, and leave the woman alone."

"But I didn't—"

They cut him off before he could get in another word. "She done tuckered herself out cleaning this old place for you, and waiting on you while you were laid up in bed, the least you could do was give the lady a moment's peace."

He opened his mouth to respond, but not a word that would make any sense came to mind. They wouldn't understand his concern for her any more than he did, so he just nodded then made his way back to the kitchen.

Canna was seated at the table with Hanson, both eating sandwiches made from piles of meat and cheese and the slices of bread Canna had cut, and even some chicken salad. Canna's sandwich wasn't much to speak of, but she was eating, while Hanson's was a profound stack most men wouldn't be able to get their hands around, much less eat. He chewed with a smile on his face, and Colt couldn't help but grin back at him. Hattie had come into their lives and changed everything.

Hanson wasn't a smiler, nor a talker, and usually not sociable past the bar, and Canna would probably be sweeping instead of eating, but here they were, the three of them sitting around a kitchen table for a meal, and all because of Hattie.

"Told you she was fine," Canna muttered, her head down.

He took a seat beside Hanson. "I just needed to hear it from her, I guess."

"She'll be fine in an hour or so," Canna said, then wiped her mouth. When did she start using a napkin?

"Yeah, Patty and Lila said pretty much the same."

"They said they'd fetch me if she needed somethin'," she replied.

His gaze met hers. "You take good care of her, Canna. I'm depending on you."

Canna managed to hide half her grin behind a small glass of milk. "Okay, Boss."

"And stop calling me boss," he groused, then slapped some meat on a piece of bread. He was no more the boss around The Golden Lady than the man in the moon. Hattie was the boss. Why bother to deny it?

****

A few days passed and Hattie and Canna had found a reasonable schedule to keep her health intact without so much fuss, and Colt hadn't said a word about it.

Hattie knew Canna had kept her promise, and she'd let Patty and Lila continue to think she was merely overworked. She'd heard them berate Colt the day he came to check on her, but no one else knew about her problem other than Canna. For this, she was grateful. After the revulsion her husband had for her and her disorder, she didn't think she could bear the same from Colt or the others.

They'd all settled into a nice little routine, just like a family, which brought a smile to her face. There were a few people in town that still whispered as she passed them by, but in time she believed they'd come to understand what was real and what wasn't. She was happy for the first time in a long while, and that was all that mattered.

"Where ya goin'?" Canna asked, lifting her head from the bowl of potatoes she was peeling.

"I have an appointment at the bank. I'll be back in a little while."

"What do you want me to do when I finish peeling?"

Hattie paused at the door and looked back at the young girl. "Canna, don't you have any fun with other children your age? Do you play, or well, anything? I feel like I'm using you as a servant."

The child dropped her chin to her chest and focused hard on the potato in her hand. "I ain't got no friends," she mumbled.

Hattie wasn't quite sure what to say to that, it just broke her heart. "Well then, when I get back, we can try something new. How about a cake."

She lifted a hopeful face. "Cake? Can it be chocolate?"

"Chocolate it is."

With Canna's smiling face fresh in her mind's eye, Hattie left for the bank. She needed to make absolutely certain her money was safe and that her trust funds would be deposited in a timely fashion. After the issues she'd had with her husband, thankfully learned early on in their married life, she kept an eagle eye on all of her funds. She refused to allow anyone to ever take advantage of her again.

When Colt had learned where she was going that afternoon, they agreed to meet and to set up a joint account for the saloon until the ownership issue could be resolved. They'd intended to do it ages ago, but it seemed, of late, that whenever she wanted to do something, like dust shelves or arrange inventory, either he or Hanson were suddenly by her side, which meant the chore took twice as long as it should have. Men tended to be more in the way when cleaning and organizing were involved.

She could only assume that her daily rests had somehow convinced the men that she was fragile. Even Lila and Patty seemed to go a bit out of their way to be helpful. It was all very annoying, but she did her best to appear more than capable, which she was, and to do as many chores and tasks without their assistance. Canna and she had become quite adept at keeping their list secret. This morning, however, Colt had intercepted her in the kitchen with a direct question as to her plans for the day. Although she prevaricated on the details, she did mention the bank.

She entered the bank several minutes before their agreed upon time and was immediately ushered into Mr. Fairfax's office.

"Can I get you some coffee, Mrs. Baker?"

"No thank you, Mr. Fairfax. But while we wait for Mr. Coltrane, I would like to settle a few things regarding my personal account."

"Of course, ma'am. Whatever you need we will accommodate you."

She liked Mr. Fairfax. He seemed honest and knowledgeable regarding trust funds and other banking oddities regarding her inheritance, but she had to be certain of a few things. "I want to be clear that under no circumstances are any monies to be added or removed from my account at any time without my personal acknowledgement."

"That's a rather odd request. I mean to say, that of course we would never do anything—"

"Mr. Fairfax, my inheritance is extremely complicated. There are countless transactions that take place between banks, agencies and organizations that often appear to happen without my knowledge. Although what I have here is a simple bank account for daily living expenses and such, I just wish to make it clear that I personally oversee each and every transaction that takes place in *all* of my accounts. No one, I repeat, no one, not even my own lawyers, have any control over my funds. They dictate that of my father's last wishes in regards to my trust fund, but that is all. Do you understand?"

"Yes, ma'am. I understand completely and you can rely on us in whatever capacity you require."

"Thank you, I'm glad that's settled."

There was a knock at the door and Colt stepped

inside. Within a few minutes, they had their new account set up, then left the bank.

Hattie ignored the outright stares as Colt escorted her down the boardwalk toward the saloon. They were so ridiculous, but she had found that many understood their situation and had been rather pleasant to her. She would even venture to say that she'd made a friend in Mrs. Gladstone, the hotel owner's wife.

"I'm surprised that Fairfax wasn't shocked by our bit of business," Colt said.

"I suspect that is due to the conversation we had prior to your arrival."

Colt chuckled. "I bet that was a dilly."

Hattie opened her mouth to protest, but ended with a grin at his wink. He already knew her so well, it was uncanny.

And yet, he was still a bit of a mystery to her. He was no ordinary gambler, of that she was certain. But how had he gotten to this point in his life? Why did he choose to be a gambler?

"I hope you haven't had to listen to any nastiness from others," he said, leading her down the small side street, no doubt noticing the stares.

"The hotel manager seemed fine with our arrangement, knowing that he was gaining a long-term resident that paid regularly, but the general store, well that is still a problem. I just don't understand why that man has to be so nasty, and not just to me, but to everyone."

"Jenkins can be a curmudgeon and a misogynist. But as much as I hate to say it, if you'd go back to New York, there'd be no gossip."

She paused and looked at him, her heart in her

throat. "You want me to leave?"

"No! Of course not! I just hate anyone saying anything bad about you. And I don't want you to leave just because you take care of all of us, I want—that is to say, I like—I don't want you to leave." He took her by the elbow and continued their walk toward the kitchen door.

Her heart beat rapidly against her chest, and she knew then that she could and would probably fall deeply in love with this man. Be it friend or more, it didn't matter. She believed deep down in her heart that he truly cared, and that meant the world to her.

"I'm—um—glad to hear it. And to be honest, I really don't care what they think," she said. "I've let others influence me before, and I won't allow that again. Never—ever—again."

Colt paused at the back door to the kitchen. "Your husband?"

"Yes. I'm afraid my husband was—unkind."

"I won't pry, Hattie, but any man that would treat you poorly, is no man. He's a swine." He lifted her gloved hand to his lips and kissed it. Oh, how she wished her hands had been bare.

The door flew open and Canna stood there, here face red from crying and her eyes wide.

"What is it? What's wrong?" Hattie asked, as she and Colt rushed inside.

Colt gripped Canna by the upper arms. "Whatever it is, just tell us what happened."

Tears slipped from her eyes, as her bottom lip trembled. "I-I can't." She cast a pleading look to Hattie.

"Colt, I think you need to see to your work in the office." It was apparent that whatever was troubling the child, she couldn't say it in front of Colt.

"Not until I get to the bottom of this!"

The look on his face, the face of a half-crazed father wanting to kill whoever dare mess with his daughter, made Hattie's chest hurt. This man wasn't just a gambler and a gentleman. He was a father to an orphan, a friend to the lost and alone. She knew there were dark days behind Mr. Hanson, and that Patty and Lila had nowhere else to go. And then there was herself, a woman he could've sent packing if he'd wished it. He never had to agree to her terms, but he did anyway. He'd give a starving man his last crust of bread.

She crossed to him and placed her hand on his arm where he still gripped Canna. She and Hattie did share her secret, so she knew that whatever the trouble was, if Canna wanted it kept private, Hattie would do as she asked. "I think this is something I need to handle," she said.

"But—"

"I promise to call you if need be."

Colt's panicked breathing slowed, his worry softened only a bit, but he managed to calm himself enough and release Canna. "I'll be in my office."

He moved to the doorway and paused with a glance back at Hattie and Canna, then disappeared.

She turned to the young girl. "Well now, what seems to be the trouble, sweetheart?"

"You—I—you don't know—"

"I know that you're a very bright young lady, and that between us, whatever the issue is, we'll solve it."

"You know?" Canna's voice cracked.

Hattie placed her reticule on the table. "Yes, dear, of course I do. I have since the day I met you. And so does

Colt and Mr. Hanson, and Lila and Patty do as well. I assumed you knew that we were aware of you being a girl. But no matter. Now sit, and let's talk about what's troubling you. I promise whatever it is, you can trust me to keep it between us if that's what you want."

Hattie started to remove her gloves, but was halted when Canna grabbed her around the waist and buried her smudged face to her breast while hugging the daylights out of her.

"Oh Canna, it's alright. There, there."

Tears moistened Hattie's jacket as she held the child and brushed her hand over her head. She'd always wanted a child, and it would appear that she had one. Canna needed a mother, and she would give her all that she could, all that Canna would allow her to give.

From the corner of her eye, she saw Colt steal a glance around the door, and she gave a slight shake of her head. He nodded with a grim frown then disappeared, hopefully content to know that she would inform him of whatever it was that was bothering the girl. Because in some odd way they were Canna's parents.

She almost laughed at the bizarre twist her life had taken, but felt, as she continued to sooth Canna's tears, that her father would approve of her unusual choices.

The girl's tears slowed, and she managed to get her to sit down. "Now, tell me what's wrong. Has someone done something?"

"No." She sniffled and wiped her nose on the back of her sleeve.

Hattie handed her a handkerchief. "Young ladies use these," she said with a small smile.

Canna half giggled.

Hattie sat beside her. "Now tell me what the trouble

is."

"I've—I've come into my courses."

With a heavy sigh and a deep breath, Hattie sat back with a relieved smile. "Ah, I see. That is very distressing when unprepared. But you know what they're about then?"

"Yes, ma'am."

"Canna, how old are you?"

"I'll be fifteen—I think—come October."

"Well, now, not to worry. All will be well."

Hattie began to explain a few things to the now young woman, and how to deal with the problem. Once done, she made her way to speak to Colt before he walked the soles off his shoes pacing in the office.

Colt pounced on Hattie the minute she walked in. The wait had been brutal. If someone had done anything to that kid, he had no qualms about hunting them down and killing them. In his life, prior to being a gambler, he had seen some depraved people, had managed to put a few of them behind bars, but never had anyone come close to hurting someone he cared for. Canna wasn't a blood relative, but she was his kid in every other way and he'd die defending her.

"What happened?" he asked, dreading the answer.

She grinned, and said, "Nothing you need to do anything about. No one to pummel or kill."

He paced to his desk and sat on the corner, his heart slowing to an almost normal rhythm. "Then what in hell was all that about?"

"Ah, how to put this delicately. Canna has become a young woman."

"And I don't need to kill anyone?"

Hattie made a face at him.

"What? Oh! You mean…"

"Yes, and don't be so relieved. Now we have to worry over her looking more and more like a woman. That female growth spurt you were so concerned about."

He ran his fingers through his hair, the old problem of what to do with Canna resurfacing.

With a groan, he shook his head. "I don't know what we're going to do with that kid."

"I'll talk to her some more today and see what it is she wants to do while we're baking a cake. Perhaps she has some ideas, one never knows."

With a chuckle, he shook his head and smiled at her. "You are an optimist, Hattie."

"Always." She smiled and sailed out of the office.

He couldn't believe he was thanking God for bringing her into his life, when not so long ago, he was cursing Him.

****

"Is that all there is to it?" Canna asked.

"That's all there is to it," Hattie said with a small laugh. "Cooking isn't as difficult as people think it is, but it does require patience and an enjoyment in the process. But I must admit that desserts are my favorite thing to make."

They moved the dirty bowls and things to the sink and started to clean up after placing the cake pans in the oven. Hattie washed while Canna dried.

"Canna, now that you're a young woman, there are some things I'd like to talk to you about."

"I know about boys, if that's whatcha' mean."

The faint blush to Canna's cheeks told Hattie that she knew more than was probably proper for a girl her age, but what else could she expect after what the child had gone through? After all, she did live in a saloon with a pair of soiled doves. There was no telling the things she'd seen or heard in her young life.

"No, not about boys exactly. But about being a young woman." Hattie paused in her washing. "What I mean to say is, how much longer do you intend on pretending to be a boy? Eventually people are going to notice."

Her gaze fell to the bowl she was drying, her fingers rubbing at an imaginary spot. "Don't matter much."

"You mean it doesn't matter. But don't you want to have dresses and other things, and eventually have a beau?"

Her gaze lifted to Hattie's. "Wouldn't make a difference if I did on account of my paw. He owed everyone in town money and even tried to swindle a few. When folks got wise to him, he figured he'd travel faster without me." She went back to drying the bowl, her voice breaking just the tiniest bit. "Most folks that remember him call me orphan trash no how. A pretty dress ain't gonna change their minds."

She quickly placed the bowl on the shelf and hurried from the kitchen leaving Hattie with tears standing in her eyes. There had to be a way to make it so that child had a better life than the one she'd been left by her father.

"There just has to be," she murmured, more determined than ever.

Chapter Five

After several weeks of trying to find a way to help Canna, Hattie all but gave up. She'd even tried to convince her to move in with her at the hotel, thinking that would be a small step in the right direction, but she refused. Apparently, the hotel manager wasn't anymore fond of her than Mr. Jenkins.

Hattie lifted her head from the column of numbers she was working on to watch her young friend. She'd set up a small table and chair for her to sit at and work on her reading and writing skills while Hanna worked on the saloon's books. Canna really was a fast learner.

With a smile at how hard Canna appeared to be concentrating on her work, Hattie rose and placed the ledger on the shelf. She straightened the few others and dislodged a small journal. Catching it before it could fall to the floor, a piece of paper slipped from inside and fluttered to her feet. She lifted the page and started to return it to the journal when she noticed the heading. It was a legal document.

Although she felt she was prying, as it seemed the journal was of a personal nature, she couldn't seem to stop herself from reading it. As her gaze scanned the words, she realized it was the original agreement between Mr. Cofield and Mr. Poole regarding the saloon. Relieved to have not stumbled on something of Colt's that was personal, she started to put it back where it was when the signatures at the bottom of the document made her breath catch for a moment.

That was definitely Mr. Cofield's signature, she'd seen it a hundred times, but that was not Mr. Poole's. At least, not the signature on her bill of sale.

She quickly shoved the journal back onto the shelf and hurried to the safe. With a jerk, she opened the door and withdrew her bill of sale and compared the signatures.

Her fear was realized. The signatures did not match. Although feeble as it was, she'd hoped her claim was valid, but it was not to be. Her husband had been cheated.

What do I do now?

She'd put all her energy into work and forcing herself not to think on what would happen if she had no claim to the saloon. She had no other plans, no other ideas for a new life. She now had no future and nowhere else to go.

She fell back against the leather chair and closed her eyes, holding back tears begging to be freed. She didn't want to leave, but what else was there for her to do? The Golden Lady was not hers, no matter how much it felt like home.

"Hattie?"

She opened her eyes to find Canna leaning over her, a worried frown on her young face.

What will become of Canna if I leave?

Of course, she could try and convince her to go with her, but doubted she would. Willow Bend was her home.

"Are you alright? Do you need me to get your medicine?" Canna asked.

Hattie couldn't speak, she hurt so much for all things she'd wanted and lost, for the things she'd come to love in Willow Bend.

"Medicine? What medicine?" Colt stopped in front of the desk, a confused and worried look on his face. "What's going on? Hattie, are you sick?"

She shook her head ever so slightly, knowing that if she spoke there would be tears in her voice and the ones in her eyes would begin to fall at will.

"She's fine, she just needs to rest. I can handle this," Canna said.

"I'm going for the doctor."

"She doesn't want the doctor," Canna snapped back.

"Well, she's going to get one."

Canna waved her hand in his face. "Just go play with your cards or something. She'll be fine."

Colt leaned over the girl. "You've developed a smart mouth, kid. I ought to take you over my knee."

"As if you could."

"I could and I will if you don't watch that mouth of yours. You're not too old to spank."

"I'm fine," Hattie said. "I don't need the doctor, really." But they paid her no attention.

Canna fisted her hands on her hips and stuck her nose up in Colt's face. "You don't even know how old I am, *old man.*"

"Old! Why you little…"

Hattie watched them argue over her for a moment more, then quietly slipped out the door. She needed to think and couldn't do that with their continued bickering.

A sad smile stole over her lips, as she stepped into the hall. They both cared about her, they cared very much. And they cared about one another. They really were her family and she didn't want to leave them. She couldn't leave them, but what was she going to do now?

She started for the kitchen, then paused. Patty and Lila were in there having their afternoon meal, and the last thing she wanted to do was try and be chatty.

Glancing over her shoulder down the hall, she considered hiding in the storage room for a while, but it was clear that Mr. Hanson was in there gathering what he needed for the night ahead in the saloon.

She considered the upstairs room, but would have to pass the office doorway to get there, and it sounded as if Colt and Canna's argument was coming to a head. They'd be looking for her, no doubt, and she wanted— needed to be alone to think.

She turned away and went to the end of the hall toward the vacant shop next door. With a quick twist of the knob, she was inside and closed the door behind her. Peace settled over her in the empty space. Muffled sounds bled through the walls and boarded up windows, but they were disconnected from her. It was almost soothing, like waves on a lonely beach.

The walls were lined with empty shelves, save for the thick layer of dust. Until now, she'd not realized the store windows wrapped around the side of the building, and if it weren't for the boards, sunlight would fill the room. It was a very nice space for a store, and she wondered for half a moment who the owner was and why they'd chosen to leave.

Her skirts stirred the dust from the floor, as she crossed to stand by the bank of windows. Hugging herself, she leaned against the wall and peered through the boards covering the glass. Dust motes danced in the sunbeams breaking through the cracks, and she emersed herself in thought. She had a problem to solve, and had no idea how to do it or where to start.

The facts were plain. She was not the owner or even the half-owner of The Golden Lady. She had no home to go back to, no actual home here in Willow Bend, nothing to claim as hers. All she had was this unlikely group of people she considered family. Canna was the daughter she had always wanted, Mr. Hanson was a bit like an older brother, while Patty and Lila were her unusual sisters, and Colt...

A long, heavy sigh escaped her lips. There was little doubt about it. She was in love with the man. He was more than charming and handsome, he was kind and generous. He was everything she'd wished her husband had been, but now he knew she was sick. Canna wouldn't be able to keep the secret. Colt would demand to know why she had medicine at the ready. And when he knew it all, there would be the same look of revulsion she'd seen on her husband's face when he'd learned of her illness. It would break her heart.

She rubbed her brow against the conundrum before her. None of these things solved her problem. She'd come to Willow Bend for a new life. One with new goals and a new purpose. Although they were like family to her, she still had nothing to claim as her own. No home, no plans, and no future to speak of.

"What am I going to do?" she murmured.

****

Colt was pulling out his hair trying to find Hattie. Canna had checked the upstairs, while he checked the saloon and the kitchen. He'd even searched behind the boxes in the store room. If he had to make a complete fool of himself and search the entire town he would, but he couldn't understand how she could disappear so completely in a matter of minutes.

"Any luck?" Canna said, bounding down the backstairs.

"No. I've looked everywhere," he said, spinning around to go back into the office when out of the corner of his eye he remembered the door at the end of the hall. It was the last place to look.

Colt rushed down the hall and burst into the vacant shop with Canna on his heels. They both fell still at the sight of Hattie leaning against the far wall, her arms wrapped around herself.

"I'm fine," she said, not turning to look at them.

Canna started to move toward her, but Colt stopped her with a hand on her shoulder and a shake of his head. With a deep frown, she returned a hesitant nod and left, closing the door behind her.

"Hattie?" he asked.

She lifted her head from the wall and looked at him. "It's called epilepsy."

His heart sank to his stomach and he swallowed hard. He'd heard of the disorder, and had come in contact with other lawyers who'd dealt with families committing the ill person to an asylum, but he'd never actually known anyone with the affliction.

She looked back to the window with a sardonic laugh. "It's not contagious, so you needn't fear for your life."

"I know what it is." He eased closer.

"I didn't always have it," she said. "When I was twelve years old, I was in a carriage accident. It took the life of my mother and left me in a comma for several days. When I awoke, I seemed fine at first, then some months later I had a seizure. I fell to the floor and twisted and writhed like I'd been possessed by a demon. Or so they told me. My father spared no expense in his search for a cure. I've seen doctors from around the country and even Europe, all with the same result. I have to live with the seizures for the rest of my life and there's nothing I can do about it."

She held herself tighter. "So now you know my secret. Now you know why I don't need a doctor."

Colt wasn't sure what to say. He wanted to hold her, he wanted to fix it, he wanted—he didn't know what he wanted, but he hated seeing her suffer like this. "So that's why you take rests every day."

"Yes. That and bromide from time to time. I've not had a bad seizure in a very long time, but there's always the possibility. Canna was with me when I had a small seizure a several weeks ago. That's why she knows." She let out half a chuckle. "She keeps a very close eye on me."

"You could've told me. You didn't need to keep it a secret from me."

She shook her head, but didn't to look at him. "I couldn't take the chance that you'd be disgusted. To see the look on your face as I'd seen so many times on others. To be treated like a leper, to be told I was mad and should be put away." She rested her head against the wall, her gaze seeming to look at nothing in particular. "Maybe they're right. Maybe it would be best if I was put away somewhere."

He gripped her arms and spun her around, her startled gaze colliding with his. "Don't talk like that! You are a beautiful, intelligent woman that can do whatever you put your mind to. You have more heart, more understanding, more talent than any woman I have ever known. Your illness does not define you."

"Then you don't—you're not—" Her eyes glistened in the dim light, disbelief evident on her face behind her quivering smile. "You don't think I'm some sort of freak?"

He let out a pent-up breath and smiled. "You're a wonder, Hattie. A beautiful, fabulous, magnificent wonder, and I'll always be grateful for the day you marched into The Golden Lady."

"The Golden Lady," she said, her voice but a whisper as her quivering smile fell. She pulled from his arms and moved across the room. "There's something I have to tell you." She turned and looked at him, tears beginning to slide down her cheeks. "I'm not half owner of The Golden Lady."

He refrained judgement, not liking where this was going. It would kill him inside if he discovered she'd lied all this time about her dead husband and his supposed ownership of the saloon. "And you know this how?"

"I found this," she said, holding out a piece of paper to him. "It's the original agreement between Mr. Cofield and Mr. Poole."

He took the paper and gave it a glance. "So?"

She looked up at him, her hands wringing before her. "Mr. Poole's signature is nothing like the one on my bill of sale. I was afraid, when I'd seen your bill of sale, that my claim could be false, but I dismissed it. I wanted—needed to be here. To do something with my life. But now—" She dropped her hands in defeat. "It's over. I have no claims of any kind on The Golden Lady."

He smiled and shook his head. The things women thought were important, the things she thought she had to keep a secret, boggled his mind. "It doesn't matter. Only the name has changed, nothing else."

"No, everything has changed, don't you see? I can't be just a cook or a bookkeeper, any more than I could be a socialite or a wife. I want more. I'm capable of more."

A wave of panicked swept through him. "You're leaving me?" He clamped his eyes closed and shook his head. "I mean us. You're leaving us?"

She reached out and touched his cheek and he opened his eyes. "I don't want to leave. This has become my home, you—you and the others are my family now, but I need more."

He clasped her wrist where she still cradled his cheek. "Whatever you want me to do, I'll do it. I'll even sign the damn saloon over to, if you'll stay."

"You'd really do that for me, wouldn't you?"

"Of course I would."

A bright tear-filled smile spread across her lips. "Maximillian Coltrane, I adore you."

Colt's heart pounded harder in his chest. "Words like that are liable to get you kissed, Hattie."

Her smile turned mischievous. "If I say them again, will you kiss me?"

He needed no further invitation.

Her lips were sweet and soft, and he lingered, savoring every moment. The shy tentative return of his kiss, proved to him that her husband had never treated her as the true treasure she was.

"I'd like to continue this, but I don't think it's wise," he whispered against her trembling lips.

"Just a little more. Please. I've never been properly kissed before and I'd like it to last."

"Hattie, this isn't the last time I'll kiss you." He pressed one last kiss to her lips, knowing if he continued, he would find himself carrying her to his bedroom.

"Now, what do you think of becoming a true half-owner of a saloon?"

She giggled softly, her head nestled beneath his chin. "I thought you said you'd sign the whole thing over."

"That I did, but I wouldn't want to run the risk of you getting tired of me and tossing me out on my ear."

She lifted her head with a bright laugh. "I don't think that's a possibility, but I do like how you plan ahead. You're a better business man than I gave you credit for."

With a broad grin, he said, "I thank you, madam, but you've not yet agreed to my proposal."

Her smile slipped. "Half-owner."

"I see the wheels turning, Hattie. Do you not want to be half-owner?"

"Well, it's just that I'd had plans for the saloon."

"Ah yes, your restaurant. I still don't think that a restaurant like the one you had in mind would work in Willow Bend."

She dropped her gaze to his chest and fingered his tie. "No, after having been here a while I agree, but I have to have something that's my own." She jerked her chin up and looked at him. "I know that sounds incredibly selfish but—"

He pressed a quick kiss to her lips. "Shh. I understand. We'll think of something that will work. Something you can do that will satisfy the determined entrepreneur in you while keeping The Golden Lady intact."

With a happy sigh, she pressed her face to this chest as he held her tight in his arms. "I just wish my original idea had worked."

He chuckled beneath his breath. "I just had an image

of Jenkins eating in your fancy restaurant. That is not a pretty picture. He'd ruin the place for all your customers."

She laughed. "Oh, how awful! He'd run everyone out just by the sheer smell of him."

"He'd curdle your cream, that's for sure."

They laughed for a good minute or two when Hattie went still.

"Now what? I swear, woman, you have the disposition of a chameleon. I can't keep up."

"Jenkins."

"What about him?"

"His general store sells mostly tack and tools, basic groceries and textiles, and a few decent items other than the absolute necessities."

"So?"

She spun away and kicked up a swirl of dust. "Don't you see? I could open a store, right here. One that sells the finer quality items that ladies want for their homes and kitchens, and their personal ablutions." She hurried to a corner near the back. "I could even put in a baker's cabinet here and sell pastries and sweets. And over here I could set up a small tea serving area for the ladies. I could call it the Willow Bend Emporium."

Colt watched as she hurried around the vacant shop, her eyes bright with excitement, her lips still full and red from his attentions, and he didn't think he'd ever seen a more beautiful sight.

"Oh, but the saloon. Do you think ladies would shop beside a saloon?"

"I think the ladies of Willow Bend will shop wherever they can to get what it is they want. The Golden Lady only gets rough closer to evening, and that isn't when they'll be shopping. And none of them have any fondness for Jenkins. It would be an improvement regardless of its location."

"I think you may be right. But what about the owner? I have to find out who owns the store. What if he won't sell or lease it to me?"

He pulled her back into his arms with a chuckle. "I know he'll let you have it, and he'll make any changes you want, no matter the extravagance."

"How do you know?"

"Because I own it, Hattie."

"You?"

"Yes, me." He pecked a small kiss to the tip of her nose, unable to resist the adorable shocked expression on her face. "When the original owner decided to go west for gold, I bought it. I didn't want just anyone attached to the saloon through a back door."

"Oh, Colt. You really are a very good businessman."

She gave him a kiss, one that lingered, and he had to make himself end it before things got out of hand and that idea of his bedroom took root.

"I think there's something you should also know about this shop." He took hold of her hand and led her up a small set of stairs in the tiny kitchen in the back. "This was used for storage, but we could renovate it and you'd have a place to live. I know how much you hate living in the hotel, and you would then have a place to call your own. A home."

"Oh my, it's massive." She rushed around the space and walked off several feet. "There's enough to make two bedrooms and a sitting area."

"Two?"

She smiled wide. "If I'm lucky and very convincing,

I think I could get Canna to live here with me."

"Now that sounds like a very good idea," he said, relieved to know that both of them would be here, right where they belonged and all while being totally respectable.

"Yes, she can live here, and—"

"And what?"

"I have toyed with an idea for some time and now with all this, I think I have the perfect plan."

"Are you going to enlighten me?"

She threw her arms around his neck and kissed him, long and hard. Well, almost respectable.

"Let's go tell Canna about your new plan," he said, whispering the words against her lips.

"Mmm, but it's so nice right here."

There was no doubt in his mind that her husband had no idea how to treat a lady, much less his own wife. One that was beautiful, kind, and most definitely desirable. "Hattie, if we keep on like this, I can't be held responsible for what happens."

With a heavy sigh, she pulled away. "I suppose you're right."

He took her hand and they started down the stairs. "Now what's this plan of yours?"

She smiled at him and squeezed his hand. "You'll see."

They made their way to the kitchen where Canna was fixing a fresh pot of coffee. Patty and Lila were putting away the cleaned dishes from their meal, and Hanson was just finishing up at the table.

"Good, you're all here," Colt said, ushering Hattie into the room. "We have a bit of news."

They all looked back and forth between him and

Hattie, and he held in his chuckle. He'd love to tell them what it was they were obviously thinking, but he was going to keep his relationship with the beautiful widow all to himself for the time being. He wasn't sure where it would lead and didn't want to stir up a bunch of gossip about them, even if it was just their makeshift family.

"Hattie, you have the floor," he announced, and stepped aside. The looks grew more confused, making him smile all the wider.

Hattie cleared her throat. "I am not the half-owner of The Golden Lady. Nor am I the sole owner. My husband was apparently cheated."

Canna was the first to start to speak, but Hattie held up her hand and silenced them all.

"Therefore," she continued. "I have decided to open a small store and tea room next door in the vacant space. A store that will cater more to the ladies of the town, and yet still allow me to hold to some of my original idea of opening a restaurant."

"Then you're not leaving?" Canna asked, her voice tense.

"I am not leaving. I—Colt has agreed to allow me to renovate the upstairs above the shop and make it my home."

"Does this mean—well—I for one would like it if you kept cooking for us, ma'am," Hanson said.

She patted his shoulder with a nod. "Of course I will. The kitchen next door isn't big enough to cook family meals in as well as dine, so I intend to make it into a kitchen suited for a dessertery of sorts. That way I can cook the confections there to supply the emporium without upsetting our living arrangements here."

"Thank God for that," Patty said.

"You said it," Lila replied. "We're not bad cooks, mind ya, but we just don't care for it."

"You got that right," Patty said with a boisterous laugh, as they walked out of the kitchen.

"I think that's a grand idea, and I thank you, ma'am," Hanson said, and rose to place his plate beside the sink. Canna snatched it up and washed it immediately. It was dried and back in the cupboard before he could get through the door.

"You're awfully quiet, kid," Colt said. He knew losing Hattie would be a big blow to her, and could feel the relief from across the room when she said she was staying, but he couldn't figure out why she was so silent on the matter.

He glanced at Hattie and she shrugged, just as baffled as he was by the kid's behavior.

"Canna, I um, have something else I need to speak to you about," Hattie said.

The young woman turned, her eyes shining with unshed tears, but she sniffed and acted as if they weren't there. "Okay, shoot."

"Have a seat," Colt said, holding out two chairs, one for each of them. Once they were seated around the table, he sat next to Hattie and waited to hear what this plan of hers was. He hoped it wouldn't backfire on her.

"Canna, I would very much like it if you would come and work with me in the emporium."

The kid glanced at Colt, her tears gone, and he gave her an encouraging nod.

"Sure, I can do that," she said.

"I'm glad, but you must understand there will have to be some changes," Hattie said.

"What kind of changes?"

Hattie cast a small nervous glance at Colt, then continued. "You'll have to clean yourself up and wear a dress."

Canna clenched her jaw and looked away. "I already told you why I can't do that."

"Well, I have this idea. A desire, really, so please hear me out."

The kid sat stoically silent.

"To set up the shop properly, I'm going to need to travel to New York. I have some things there in storage that I will want in our living quarters and I'll need to set up some connections with suppliers and such."

"Our quarters?"

"Yes, dear. Our quarters. I thought that you could go with me to New York as Canna, then come back as Anna."

Colt sat on the edge of his seat and could feel the anticipation sizzling in Hattie beside him. It was a fantastic idea. He only hoped the kid would go for it.

Canna's jaw worked, like she either wanted to say something or spit, Colt couldn't tell.

She shook her head. "I have to earn—"

"You already have," Hattie rushed to say. "You've taken care of me, helped me. You do anything anyone ever asks of you, and you'd be working in the emporium."

"You deserve it, kid. Don't pass this by. It isn't every day you hold a royal flush," he said with a wink.

"My—" The kid swallowed hard. "My name really is Anna. I ain't—haven't heard anyone call me that in a long time."

With tears welling in her eyes, Hattie took hold of Canna's hand. "There's just one other thing. We can either tell people you're a daughter of a friend who has come to live with me or I could adopt you. Either way, you'd have your own room and your own clothes and things. Just like other young girls. The decision is yours."

Canna's jaw fell open and tears seeped from the corners of her eyes. "You want me to be family?"

"You already are, dear. It would just make it legal."

The kid threw herself at Hattie, nearly toppling them both over in the chair and cried her little heart out.

Colt rose as Hattie looked up at him, tears streaming down her face. If he hadn't loved this woman before, he did now.

He stood behind the chair and squeezed Hattie's shoulders as he placed a kiss on the top of her head, then left them alone to become mother and daughter.

Chapter Six

"I look stupid."

Hattie had to blink a moment before hiding her smile. "You look fine."

She pushed the stringy hair behind Canna's ears then looked hard at the girl for the first time. She was very pretty once you got past the smudges of dirt and the messy hair. And there was a very nice figure hiding amidst her baggy clothes.

"Then I feel stupid," Canna said.

"Don't be silly. Now turn around and let me see how it fits."

Hattie had usurped the empty bedroom in the saloon as a makeshift sewing room. A pair of her old dresses, the ones that didn't look like a widow's cast-offs, would do nicely for Canna until they could get her some new things in New York.

"Yes, this will work perfectly," she said. "I knew you and I were close in height, that a little raising of the hem would be fine and a few other alterations for your age, but the rest of you is quite a shock. I had no idea what a shapely figure you had."

"I still feel stupid."

Hattie laughed and placed another pin in her old dress. Their scheme would work. Once on the train, and well out of sight of Willow Bend, Canna would change clothes and become Anna. "We'll need to fix your hair, of course," she said as she pinned. "I'm glad you've not cut it again. I recall it was rather short when we first met."

"Long was too much trouble. But I—"

Hattie pulled the pins from her mouth and looked up at the girl. "But what?"

"I saw how pretty yours was and I wanted mine to be like that. All neat and clean and piled up proper for a lady. Patty and Lila's hair is nice, but it's not the way a lady wears it."

Hattie bit back her tears, Canna wouldn't understand the reason for them. At how much it touched her to know that the girl wanted to emulate her.

"Well, we'll wash it and see what we can do. But you'll have to stop putting that—what is it that you put in your hair to make it so stringy?"

"Ashes. I coat it in soot from the stove, same as my face and hands."

"Well, we'll have to have a look at the fully bathed young lady then, won't we?"

"But I can't let folks see me like that. Or all this," she said, lifting the skirts, "will be for nothing."

"Not to worry. Once we derive the look, you can go back to being smudged until we leave. The day we leave you will stay clean, but we'll hide you in those old clothes and you'll keep your head down. Once we get on the train and settled, we'll transform you."

"What about the other folks on the train?"

Hattie finished her pinning, then went to work sorting out what she could of the stringy mess of hair. "We'll be alone, dear. I've arranged for a special car just for us. It's a bit more than two days of travel, and I disliked traveling in the standard car. Much too noisy and uncomfortable for such a long journey."

"You know, I ain't—haven't ever been on a train."

"Then this will be a grand adventure, one filled with new experiences and new places." She smiled at the young woman and maneuvered her toward the mirror. "There now, have a look at yourself."

Canna froze, her mouth falling agape. "Is that really me?"

Hattie squeezed her arms. "Yes, dear. That's really you."

"I guess I don't look so stupid after all, huh?"

"No, you don't. You're quite lovely. But let's not let the others see. I want them to see you when you step off the train when you return as Anna. It will make the transition easier on them, help to keep the two personas separated in some way."

Canna giggled as a young girl should, warming Hattie's heart. This trip was going to be wonderful—for both of them.

There was a tap at the door.

"Just a minute," Hattie called.

Canna ducked behind the screen Hattie had the men bring in. She'd also asked them to bring in a tub for Canna to bathe in.

Hattie opened the door to Mr. Hanson and another gentleman she didn't know.

"The tub you asked for, ma'am."

"Thank you, Mr. Hanson." She motioned for them to place it in the opposite corner of the room.

They placed it where she indicated, then Mr. Hanson turned to her. "This here is Jeb Cochran. He's the town blacksmith and he owns the livery beside it."

Mr. Cochran removed his hat and gave her a slight

bow. "Ma'am."

"It's nice to meet you, Mr. Cochran. I appreciate your help with the tub."

"He made the tub, ma'am," Mr. Hanson said.

"Oh my, then I am very grateful. The ladies will enjoy it, I am certain of that."

He gave a lopsided grin and a nod, then they both disappeared through the door.

Lila and Patty had been bathing at a washstand and would surely enjoy the tub, but it was Hattie's goal to get Canna into it, fully submersing her before they left for New York.

Canna came out from behind the screen and examined the tub. "This will sure beat that cold swim in the river."

Hattie withheld her sigh of relief, not wanting to embarrass the girl. She'd hoped Canna had been bathing, after all the child didn't smell, but she wasn't sure how or where or when she did it.

"We'll have one of our own in our apartments once the renovation is complete," Hattie said.

"I know Mr. Cochran will like that. It's not every day he gets such a big job."

Hattie looked at her from the corner of her eye. "You like him. Mr. Cochran."

"Oh, yes. He's a nice man. Even though Paw owed him and everyone else in town money when he took off, Mr. Cochran let me sleep in his hay loft all the time and made sure nobody bothered me. He wasn't too keen on me moving to the saloon, but I think after he met Colt, he thought I'd be safe here."

She slipped her arm around Canna's waist, and said, "Then I like him too. And I'm very grateful to him for signing the affidavit that your father abandoned you. We need all the witnesses we can get so that we can prove to the judge in New York that I'm free to adopt you."

"Hattie, are you sure you want me to be…"

She smiled at the worried look on Canna's face. "I want it more than anything in the world," she said, brushing her finger across the child's almost clean cheek.

"But if they all know you're adopting me, then how am I going to come back as Anna?"

"I prevaricated a bit." She went on to explain at the look of puzzlement on Canna's face. "I've told them there's a chance for you to be adopted by someone in New York. I didn't say it was I who was doing the adopting. And when we return, we won't say you're my adopted daughter. We'll just say you're my daughter."

"Ohhh. You're pretty cagey, Hattie. You know, you'd put Paw to shame with your—prevaricatin'."

They both laughed then went back to work on the second dress.

****

Colt found Hattie in the saloon kitchen where she was telling the men he'd hired what she wanted done in the renovations, but they were only listening with half an ear. He'd seen her drawings, and knew what she wanted and what needed to be done, and it was no small task. The men, however, only saw the crazy female getting under foot.

"Hattie, could I talk to you in private, please?" he asked.

She sighed and cast him a scowl, but followed him to the office.

"I don't understand why they won't listen to simple instructions," she huffed.

He closed the door behind them, pulled her into his arms and silenced her with a kiss. She protested for barely half a second before returning his attentions.

"There now," he said, pulling away. "Much better."

"You kissed me to shush me."

"Yes, sweetheart I did."

"That doesn't solve the problem at hand."

He smiled. "Hattie, they know that if they don't follow the plan, I'll not only fire them, I'll ban them from the saloon. It will all get done just as you want. I promise."

"But—"

"You need to concentrate on Canna and your trip. Leave the building details to me. I know what you want, they're drawn out to the last detail. And besides, they'll listen to me. These men aren't used to women telling them what to do."

She grinned. "And you are?"

"A little. My mother, and a certain widow I know, are forces to be reckoned with. Just let me handle it. And if I get it wrong, I'll fix it. I promise."

"Well, I suppose it's for the best. I know the work won't be done by the time I return, but I was hoping to at least have them on the right track before we leave."

"It will be fine. Now, where were we," he said, and pressed his lips to hers.

****

The day for their trip finally arrived. Canna and Hattie stood on the platform filled with nervous anticipation as the train pulled to a stop before them. They'd said their goodbyes at the saloon, not wanting to attract too much because of Canna. Her face and hair were clean, her only disguise was the baggy clothes and

105

floppy hat. One good look and they'd know Canna was a she. As they'd waited for the train, Hattie made it a point to stand between her and Jeremy, who kept looking at Canna with an odd quirk to his lips.

"You're all set, ma'am. Can't believe you're taking Canna here with you. Hey Canna, I heard they got a place with all kinds of animals from 'round the world. If'n you go, would you tell me about it when you get back?" the young man asked, still trying to see Canna's face hidden beneath her hat.

"Sure," Canna mumbled.

Hattie smiled. "I'm sure Canna will have lots of stories to tell when we return."

"All aboard!"

"Have a nice trip, ma'am," the boy said.

"Thank you, I'm sure we will."

Hattie motioned for Canna to climb on to their appointed car before her, then followed. They were met by a coach attendant, the only one they would have. Hattie had arranged it all, she wanted no mistakes. Canna had to be protected, her faith in herself, and her chance for a decent future depended on it. The fewer people that new about her, the better.

The tall black man, dressed in a starched white uniform took Hattie's satchel and escorted her and Canna into their car. "Mrs. Baker, I'm Samuel Jones, I'll be your coach attendant."

"It's a pleasure to meet you, Mr. Jones. And this is Canna," she said, motioning to the young girl, who's mouth sat agape at the luxury of the car. "Once we're on our way, we'll require a bit of privacy so we can change. But I'd be ever so grateful if you could bring us some tea after a bit."

"Certainly, ma'am. I'll bring your tea as soon as we're underway, then leave you to your privacy."

"That would be perfect. Thank you, Mr. Jones."

With a slight bow, he left the car.

Hattie pulled off her gloves and removed her hat. Canna remained in her attire while they sat in the station, but Hattie knew she was eager to discard the boyish façade once and for all.

"Well, what do you think so far?" Hattie asked.

"Hattie, are you rich?"

She laughed and sat down in one of the plush chairs, happy that her inheritance put such a wonderful smile on her soon-to-be little girl's face. Her little girl, who wasn't so little after all. But she was hers in her heart and soon it would be legal.

"Let's just say I'm not poor and leave it at that."

Canna ran her hand over the plush squabs with a giggle. "This really is an adventure."

"You think this is something, wait until you see New York."

The train tugged away from Willow Bend and Canna sat with her head in her hands as she watched it disappear behind them. "It's kind of sad."

"I suppose it is in a way," Hattie replied. "It's the end of one stage of your life and the beginning of a new one. So it carries a mixture of feelings."

Canna tossed away her ragged hat and coat with a smile. "I think I'll concentrate on the beginning and not the ending."

"Bravo," Hattie said with a wide smile.

Mr. Jones arrived with their tea. Hattie could see the surprise in his eyes at the sight of Canna without her hat and coat, and a small smile tipped the edge of his lips.

He was trained well to mask his emotions, but she had to bring him into their scheme, to be sure that he would say nothing to anyone from Willow Bend or elsewhere.

"Well, Mr. Jones. Do you think we can turn this caterpillar into a butterfly?"

He held fast to his nearly imperceptible smile. "I don't think you'll have any trouble with that, ma'am."

She laughed and gave him a conspiratorial wink, that pulled that small smile into a big one. "I'm glad you think so. I do request, however, that you keep this transformation to yourself."

"I won't breathe a word of it, ma'am. Pull the bell cord if you should need anything else and I'll be here fast as can be."

She thanked him and he left them to their privacy, and to the birth of Anna Baker.

****

The progress on the soon-to-be emporium and living quarters were moving along at a good clip. Colt was examining the detail the men were putting into place in the shop area when he overheard a couple of them talking. Talking about his ladybird, and how cozy it would be for them to sneak around when no one could see.

His stomach burned and his head pounded with rage. The whole town would think similar thoughts. Hattie knew it would be difficult, but he'd never expected it to sound so disgusting. She'd heard some whispers since the day she'd arrived, but this was far worse than he'd ever imagined.

The pair of men fell silent when they noticed him, the worried look on their faces of what he might do evident.

He clenched his jaw and took a deep breath. "I'll just pretend I didn't hear that. But if I hear another word like it again, there'll be hell to pay."

He spun on his boot heel and stormed from the shop, down the hall, and slammed his office door. Pouring himself a tall drink, he had to force his nerves to calm. The world would never believe them, regardless of whether or not they had a tryst. It was obvious he cared for her, and Hattie—well, Hattie cared about everyone. He'd walked her back to the hotel so many times, the whole damn town thought he was sweet on her. Which he was, but to hear them talk about her like she was some sort of floozy burned a hole in his gut.

After another drink, his nerves calmed, but for the remainder of the day his mind kept returning to the repulsive words he'd overheard.

"Colt, you okay?" one of the regulars asked, as Colt sat stock still holding the deck of cards.

"Sorry, gents," he said with a false smile. "I'm somewhat distracted this evening."

He passed the deck and rose to go to the bar.

One of the men laughed and said, "Yeah, you got yer mind on that slip of calico what's leadin' you around by yer pecker."

Colt pulled the man to his feet, his chair toppling to the floor, while he fisted his hands in his shirt. The room fell still. It was if the world was holding its breath.

He pressed his face close to the cowhand. "Not another word or you're a dead man."

"I was just joshin'. I swear I didn't mean nothin' by it. I swear."

Colt shoved the fool away, then stormed from the saloon. He couldn't go on like this or he'd kill someone.

With Hattie living within spitting distance of a saloon, his saloon, there was no way to avoid the unpleasantness. Although he enjoyed his life as the black sheep of the family, had walked away from their high society digs, his post as an attorney in his father's practice, the false faces, the rich who thought they could get away with murder, he was still a gentleman inside.

The sun was setting and it looked mighty nice at the end of the street, so he decided to talk a walk, maybe all the way to the river. Listening to the water rush around the bend would help him think on what to do next.

After rambling around town for nearly an hour, he came to a stop across from The Golden Lady and lit a cheroot. Leaning against a post, his gaze went to the windows above Hattie's emporium, soon to be her home. He was doing her a great disservice letting her set up shop next door, live next door.

When she returned, they couldn't go on as before, and he knew what he had to do.

****

"We're pulling into New York, Mrs. Baker," the coachman said. "I'll just take your bags here and have them ready to pass on to the porter."

"Thank you." She turned to look at Anna where she fidgeted with her skirts. "What do you think, Mr. Jones? Have we succeeded?"

He smiled wide. "Without a doubt, ma'am."

"You see, Anna? You look fine."

"You're sure, Mr. Jones? I don't look like I—like I don't belong?" she asked, her face twisted with worry.

He chuckled and shook his head. "No miss. And if'n I was you, whatever Mrs. Baker here says do, I'd do." He left with their carry-on luggage.

"You see, there's nothing to be nervous about. All will be well, trust me," Hattie said.

As they disembarked, Hattie slid a large tip into Mr. Jones' hand. "Thank you very much, Mrs. Baker. It's been a privilege to serve you."

"Thank you," she said.

As he assisted them down the steps, he cast Anna a half wink.

"Thank you," Anna said with a smile and a squeeze of his hand, then followed Hattie along the platform.

After settling into their hotel room, Hattie set out straight away to her lawyer's office. It took some time, as Anna kept stopping and staring and ogling at just about everything, until Hattie was forced to hire a cab.

"I never knew the city was so big," Anna said.

"Oh yes, and there's a lot to see and do. The park, the menagerie, the opera, the shops, the museums. After our visit with my lawyers, we can go where we like. Tomorrow, we'll go shopping for more dresses and things for you and we'll need to meet with some suppliers, but we will have time to do it all."

"I think I would like to see the animals Jeremy talked about."

Hattie smiled at her from across the coach. "You like him, don't you?"

Anna blushed a bit. "He's really good at fishing and hunting. We'd meet up sometimes—by accident by the river and such."

"And he isn't all that hard on the eyes?"

Anna studied her hands in her lap. "Do you think he'd like me like this?"

She reached across the cab and took one of her hands in hers. "I think he would be over the moon."

Her smile grew from tentative to bright and wide, warming Hattie's heart.

They arrived at the lawyers' offices and made their way inside. They were taken aback by Hattie's request for them to draw up the proper paperwork for her to adopt Anna, but knew better than to argue with her on that or just about any point.

After their legal task was complete and a hearing date set, the rest of the week filled with appointments and small excursions. She'd arranged for her furniture, which she'd had in storage, to be shipped immediately to Willow Bend. There wasn't much, but enough to fill their small apartments, including a new bedroom suit for Anna.

Hattie had never enjoyed shopping so much in her life. It was like being young again, living through Anna's eyes. Everything was a wonderful adventure.

Near the end of their trip, the day finally arrived to meet the judge and finalize the adoption papers.

"Mrs. Baker, are you quite certain you wish to do this?" the judge asked.

"Absolutely."

"And Miss Baggs, you understand that this adoption includes changing your legal name to Baker. You will no longer be associated in any way to the name Baggs."

"Yes, sir. I understand."

"Very well, then. Since we cannot establish a living parent to grant consent, and that the last known parent abandoned the child at the estimated age of ten, of which I have several signed affidavits from the various townsfolk of Willow Bend," he said, holding up the sheets of paper. "I see no reason to not grant your request. I hereby certify that Miss Anna Baggs is now to be known as Miss Anna Baker and is legally your daughter, Mrs. Baker." He signed the papers then handed Hattie a copy with a smile. "Congratulations."

"Thank you so much, Judge Collier. You've made us both very happy."

Anna looked a bit stunned as she and Hattie made their way out of the building. "Are you alright, dear?"

"I can't believe it." She looked to Hattie with tears standing in her eyes. "I've got a family. A mother. A home."

Hattie's eyes filled as well. She pulled them to a stop and retrieved her handkerchief. They both laughed as they dried their happy tears on the steps of the massive building.

"I think we should celebrate. What would you like to do?" Hattie asked.

"Could we see the menagerie again?"

"Of course." She waved down a cab and took Anna's arm. "And after we'll get ice cream."

Mother and daughter stepped into the cab and started on their new life together.

Chapter Seven

Colt waited on the platform, his stomach a bag of twisted knots. The whispers had grown worse over the few weeks she'd been away, leaving him no choice. He had to do this. It was best for both of them.

The steam spewed across the platform as the train came to a stop. Within minutes Hattie was stepping down from the train with a lovely young woman behind her. He paused for a moment, overwhelmed by the changes in the kid, and half grinned, knowing he couldn't call her kid anymore. This was a lovely young lady.

He crossed to where Hattie was making sure their bags where properly seen to.

She looked up as he approached, a wide smile on her face. "I didn't expect you to greet us."

"I figured you would have more bags than what you left with, so I thought I'd take the burden off of Jeremy here and brought a wagon."

"Oh, my yes. We did do a great deal of shopping."

"Excuse me, Mrs. Baker, but didn't Canna come back with ya'?"

She turned to the boy who had trouble keeping his eyes off the pretty young woman standing beside her. "I'm afraid not. Canna decided to stay behind. She was adopted, so I'm afraid we won't be seeing, uh, him again. But this," she said, turning to take the young woman's arm, "is my daughter, Anna. Anna, this is Jeremy Davis.

114

Anna can tell you all about the animals, Mr. Davis. It is one of her favorite sights to see in New York."

The young man snatched off his hat and blushed. "Nice to meet you, miss."

"It's nice to meet you," she replied.

All Colt could do was watch, he was so stupefied by how beautiful and refined Canna—Anna looked.

He cleared his throat and said, "Aren't you going to introduce us, Mrs. Baker?"

"I'm sorry, yes of course. Anna, this is Mr. Coltrane. You'll recall I've told you all about him."

"It's a pleasure to meet you, Miss Anna." He took her gloved hand and bowed over it.

She squeezed his fingers with a twinkle in her eye. "It's nice to finally meet you, Mr. Coltrane."

"Well ladies, why don't we get you home," he said.

Jeremy and Colt loaded their trunks onto the wagon while the ladies took their seats. Within a few minutes they were on their way down the street. Colt didn't miss the odd looks they got, the knowing grins. A few of the ladies actually put their heads together in full blown gossip. It was enough to make a man sick.

"Colt, this isn't the way to the hotel," Hattie said.

He forced a grin to his face. "Not going to the hotel. I'm taking you home, just like I said."

"Home? You mean—"

"That's right. It's all finished, just the way you wanted. I hope," he added with a rough chuckle.

He pulled the wagon to the back of the saloon and helped the ladies down from the wagon. Hanson appeared and took the first few bags from the back of the wagon, but not after a double-take at Anna.

"I'll give you a hand after they've seen what we've

done," Colt said.

Hanson nodded as Colt and the ladies went through the backdoor to the saloon. Hattie and Anna didn't even stop to remove their hat and gloves, but hurried to the shop, now partially filled with the goods she'd had shipped. Colt and Hanson had popped the crates, but left the items where they were, knowing the ladies would want to place each item. The space was what mattered, and now it was all clean and new and completely ready to open in just a matter of a few days.

Giggling like school girls, the women rushed to the kitchen where they oohed and aahed at the new stove and the long clean work table with half a slab of marble on one end. So far Colt knew he'd gotten things right, but the next test would be their living quarters.

Anna lifted her skirts and ran up the stairs like the kid he remembered, while Hattie followed at a more sedate pace, yet still in a flurry of skirts.

He followed with leaden feet, but felt instant relief when he stepped foot into their parlor. Their faces, their reaction of joy was all he needed to know he'd done the right thing by hurrying the renovation along. Cost him a pretty penny, but it was well worth it.

"Oh, Hattie, my own room. Look at my room!" Anna said with a squeal.

Hattie stood in the doorway with Colt just behind her. "It's lovely, Anna."

"How can I ever repay you? Both of you?"

"Payment already received, kid. Uh, Miss Anna," Colt said with a crooked grin.

Anna threw her arms around his waist and Hattie's, and hugged them tight. She popped up on her toes and kissed each of their cheeks before spinning away to explore her room in depth.

"Now for your room, Mrs. Baker." Colt took her by the arm and steered her to the second door. With a turn of his wrist and a small shove, the door swung open. "I hope I got this one right."

Hattie crossed the room, letting her fingers slide across the massive post of the bedframe. "It's perfect." She turned to Colt, tears welling in her throat. "Thank you for doing this. Now it feels like home."

He fidgeted where he stood at the door, an awkward smile on his face. He'd been acting strangely since they arrived, but she'd assumed it was due to this wonderful surprise. Afraid, perhaps, that she wouldn't like it.

She'd not looked forward to moving back into the hotel, nor did she care for the idea of both her and Anna traveling up and down the street for work. It was so much simpler to be where they needed to be, and it would ensure their safety. It was far too easy to work past sunset, to forget the clock when they were occupied with things, and walking back to the hotel in the dark, although they'd be together, wasn't safe.

But then why was Colt so nervous? She loved all the things he'd done for her and for Anna.

"Colt, something is troubling you. Please tell me what it is," she said, bracing herself just a bit. No one ever enjoyed receiving bad news.

"Hattie, I—" He dropped his gaze to the floor and rubbed his forehead. "I'm leaving on the afternoon train."

She swallowed the tears of gratitude that had turned to ash in her throat. "I see. And when will you return?"

"I won't be coming back. Hanson will manage the saloon and follow any instructions you wish to give, that is unless you choose to not have any further dealings with the saloon. I'll understand if that's the case."

"So, you're to be an absentee landlord then."

"Yeah. I've stayed put in one place too long. It's time for me to move on."

What he really meant was that he regretted their liaisons, their stolen kisses and touches. He no longer wanted her. His supposed wanderlust was nothing more than a ruse to try and save her feelings.

She turned to her dressing table and jerked off her gloves, wishing to speed up the unpleasant business. She couldn't bear to listen to empty platitudes. "I will continue to manage the saloon books if you wish." She laid her gloves aside then pulled her hat pin free and tidied her hair. "Now if you'll excuse me, I have quite a lot of work to do and Mr. Hanson requires your assistance."

She turned from her dressing mirror and sailed past him, her chin high, her heart racing in her chest, and her gaze straight ahead. To look at him would be her undoing. She'd had her heart broken once before, she knew she would live through it, but this time—this time it felt like death had come to call.

Colt stared after her, knowing he'd made the right decision, but felt like he'd just killed something precious. He had no words. He'd stood there like a man without a voice, and in her mind, probably a man without a heart.

He knew her husband had been cruel to her, and the indignation she'd had to endure since she was a child due to her illness, but he did have a heart and it was burning in his chest, screaming at him to go after her. And yet he remained frozen in the doorway to her room. He may have just let the best thing that ever happened to him walk out of his life.

She would remain here, and they would be friends of a sort through an occasional letter, but it would be cold and all business. Nothing but numbers and balance sheets. Perhaps the occasional tidbit of news about the others, or how the emporium was coming along, but nothing real.

There was a loud bang that shook him from his reverie and he went to help Hanson with the trunks. Then he would be on his way out of town.

****

Colt shoved his belongings into a bag, then started down the hall. Patty and Lila stood in their doorways just shaking their heads. He didn't pause, he didn't even say goodbye. He just kept walking.

Hanson's head came up from the glass he was drying as he stepped off the stairs. That piercing gaze made him pause.

"Take care of her," Colt said.

Hanson nodded and Colt crossed to the batwing doors.

"Can't help thinking this is a mistake," Hanson said.

His quiet statement brought Colt to a stop, one hand on the door, his gaze staring over it at nothing in particular, then he was gone.

This is what he had to do. He couldn't let her world be tainted by him, by what he was. Just a gambler, a saloon owner. She needed someone better than him.

****

The mood was solemn around the saloon for a spell, but everyone knew they had work to do. As for Hattie and Anna, they worked feverishly to fill the shelves and cases with the wares that arrived every day. After a week of arranging, they finally decided it was time to open the Willow Bend Emporium. Mr. Hanson was kind enough to hang a banner announcing their opening, while Hattie and Anna, who had been introduced around town to many a surprised person, talked up the emporium as much as possible. Several ladies gave them a little encouragement, but a few, those who knew Hattie better, wished them luck and said they would be overjoyed to have a new place to shop.

Opening day arrived, and with bated breath, Hattie and Anna waited for customers to come in. Within a few hours of opening, those Hattie would call friends, like the hotel manager's wife, Mrs. Gladstone came in and gushed over all the items they had on display while enjoying a lovely cup of tea and cakes. It was like a party, and once they'd left, Hattie and Anna finally began to breathe again.

The sweets case was very popular, and several of the ladies promised to buy some for special occasions, while Mrs. Gladstone was considering Hattie's proposal to buy her cakes for the hotel restaurant. It would be a wonderful side income. All in all, they hadn't made much in the way of direct sales, but with luck and some kind persuasion from their friends, other ladies would at least give them a chance.

Days turned to weeks, and the emporium was proving to be a success, but at what cost?

Hattie looked in her mirror early one morning and noted the dark circles under her eyes. When would she ever get a decent night's sleep again? Why did Colt have to haunt her every dream?

There was a tap at the door.

"Come in," she called.

"I'm going to go start coffee and breakfast. I thought I'd get a head start on the crumpets this morning before we open," Anna said. "They disappear faster than we can make them. I think the ladies just love that they're a European treat, and not so much how they taste," she said with a laugh.

"That's fine, dear."

Anna came in and rested her hand on Hattie's shoulder. "You don't look well, Hattie. Perhaps you should stay in bed today."

She patted her hand. "I'm fine. Just a bit under the weather, that's all."

Anna crouched down beside her and took her both her hands in hers. "No, it's more than that. You've had several small seizures and one that had you in bed for a full day. Please let me get the doctor."

"I don't need—"

"For me then? Please do it for me?"

Hattie looked into the sweet loving face of her daughter. She brushed the back of her fingers across her cheek, so pink and full of life. "Very well. For you. I'll go see the doctor this morning."

"No, you'll get back in bed and I'll go fetch the doctor."

Not bothering to reply or to struggle, she allowed Anna to guide her back to bed. She really was exhausted and she was right in that she'd had several seizures. But she knew the cause. She worked herself to exhaustion every day to keep her mind off of Colt, and hoping she would be so tired she'd sleep through the night and not dream about him.

But her strategy seemed to be making her more ill. Perhaps it was best if the doctor examined her. He would probably give her some laudanum to rest, then maybe she would be strong enough to gain control of her thoughts, and keep them from turning back to Colt.

Within an hour, Dr. Farleigh appeared, and just as she suspected he prescribed her a mild dose of laudanum and plenty of rest. She was to rest several times a day and not overtax herself.

Anna was the leader of the small army that refused to allow her to stray from the doctor's orders. Patty and Lila made the meals for the group, while Mr. Hanson refused to allow the piano to be played in the saloon until she'd recovered. They were all determined to have her well. She still missed Colt, her heart was still very much broken, but she was loved and cared for by the family she'd made in Willow Bend. She would get well, if not for herself, then for them.

****

Colt didn't know who the hell he ended up in Boston, but here he sat at a swanky gaming hall sipping a decent glass of whiskey and playing poker with a group of men he could easily fleece, but he didn't really give a damn if he won or lost.

Knowing he wasn't much of an opponent, he tossed in his hand and went to the bar for another drink. He wouldn't succeed in drowning his sorrows, but another belt wouldn't hurt much.

His gaze perused the room, taking note of its finery. The tables were covered with pristine green felt, not a burn or tear to be had. The roulette wheel shone brightly under the crystal chandeliers, while the dice table stools were covered with plush velvet cushions. Then there was the floor—he couldn't get over how clean it was. Barely a scuff or speck of mud to be had, and there wasn't a spittoon in sight. And the ladies, some of which he knew were peddling their wares, were dressed in the finest clothes. No one in Willow Bend would ever know what they really were. While others were upper-middle class ladies who'd come along to gamble with their men. It was all ridiculously respectable. So much so, it made his stomach churn.

His rambling around the country had gotten old before it began, and now, after weeks of traveling, he'd somehow landed in a pristine gaming hall that outshone anything he'd ever seen. And damned if all he wanted was to be back home in his scruffy old saloon with Hattie.

"A little further east than usual, aren't you?"

The familiar voice put a grin on his face and he turned. "Nice to see you too, big brother."

"Mind if I join you?"

Colt motioned the bartender for another round for the both of them.

"What are you doing this far west, Kent? Didn't think Father loosened the leash enough for you to get of New York, much less all the way to Boston."

His brother shook his head. "Not as bad as he used to be."

"Father mellowing, now there's a thought," Colt said, and took a long sip.

"So, what brings you here?"

"Same old thing, gambling, traveling, more gambling," he said, feeling the lie taste like bile on his tongue. He was running away, plain and simple. He was beginning to even think he didn't care if he picked up another deck of cards in his life. But that could just be the whiskey talking. "You here on business or pleasure?"

he asked.

His brother gave him that crooked grin he was known for. "A little bit of both. I'm here to spend some time with my fiancée's family."

"Ah, and they happen to do business with the firm. Father has it all neat and tidy."

Kent shook his head. "He wanted it, sure, but when I met her—well, let's just say I fell for her."

"I think you're actually blushing, big brother."

Kent bumped him with his shoulder in a good-natured way. "Knock it off, or I'll wipe that grin off your face."

"Pretty, no doubt," Colt said. "Smart, funny, has a proper family, of course. So, what the hell are you doing in this gaming hole? Why aren't you off with your soon-to-be bride cooing somewhere?"

He nodded toward the roulette wheel. "That's her brother. He wanted to show me Boston, but really all he wanted was to escape." He looked back at Colt with a smile. "A lot like someone else I know."

"Except he's no gambler. Roulette is how you lose your money. The house always wins."

"Yeah, but I've been watching him. He knows when to quit. I think he just enjoys the action. Cards are too tame, too quiet for him. And he's the prodigal son, so I think he's trying to let off a little steam. He'll fall in line when the time's right."

"And there we truly differ," Colt said. "I like my life the way it is. I could never fall in line and do Father's bidding. Frankly, I'm surprised you have."

"I like being a lawyer—most of the time," he added with a chuckle. "I handle corporate law now."

"Which is how you met your fiancée," Colt said,

knowing it was true.

"What about you? Mother wants grandchildren."

"You're getting married, and she already has three from George, isn't that enough?"

He laughed and shook his head. "You're her favorite, she wants little boys just like you."

Colt snorted and finished off his whiskey. "That's never going to happen." He had a little girl, one back in Willow Bend, but even now she seemed all grown up. A smile teased the corner of his lips. His mother would love Anna and Hattie. And Hattie would go toe to toe with his father.

"Want to share the joke?" Kent asked.

"Let's just say, between you and me, that I came close."

"So, what stopped you? She already married?"

He shook his head. "Widow. She's a lot like Mother, to tell the truth. All fire and spark, not afraid of anything, smart as hell, and has a stubborn streak a mile wide."

"I'd like to see you bring her home to Mother. That would be something worth seeing. So why almost? Why not walk down the aisle? Don't want to be tied down?"

He looked down into his empty glass with a sigh. "She's proper—I'm a gambler."

"You're not just any gambler. You're the son of Wentworth P. Amberson. You've got enough blue blood in your veins to float a boat."

"It's not that, it's the town she lives in. There was some unpleasant talk."

"So, you took off like always."

Colt's back snapped straight. "What's that supposed to mean?"

"It's what you do. You always run from a fight."

"You looking to start something with me?"

Kent let out a huff and shook his head. "Look, you know poker, you're damn good at it, but you are lousy when it comes to life lessons. Father was always hard on you, gave you the worst cases cause he wanted you to stand up and fight for what you wanted. But you ran instead."

Colt shook his head. "No, I wanted to be a gambler. I wanted to travel the west, explore new places."

"Okay, so you did that. Now what?" Kent placed his hand on Colt's shoulder. "Baby brother, do you love the woman?"

Colt gave a jerk of a nod.

"Then fight for her."

Colt looked down into his empty glass, the simplicity of his brother's words filling him with shame. He'd hurt Hattie when he left, he hurt them all. And all because he was a coward. Afraid to fight for the one thing that he wanted more than anything, more than being a gambler.

"Looks like my soon-to-be brother-in-law is ready to head home," Kent said. "Think about what I said, Colt. Use those excellent lawyer skills of yours and look at it from an objective point of view and you'll find the answer."

He nodded and they shook hands. "Kiss Mother for me. Tell her I'm okay."

Kent gave him a slap on the back and a wink, then went to join the young man at the door.

A few minutes after they left, Colt left as well, hoping for some quiet where he could think, but in a bustling town like Boston, that was pretty hard to come by. He felt like the world was closing in around him, suffocating him. He missed Willow Bend where he could walk to the edge of town in a matter of minutes and look out over the wilderness. The sky, black as pitch, with diamonds winking down at him, and the air clean and brisk. He could breathe there.

Perhaps that was one of the reasons he went west, to find breathing room. He could see Kent's point, but he didn't run away from his Father exactly. At the time he was running to something. Something he wanted more than anything. But this time, this time he was running. And there wasn't any place in the world he could go that would be far enough to make him forget. He'd always regret the past, the loss of Hattie and Anna in his life.

He had to go back.

Chapter Eight

"I can't believe things are going so well," Anna said. She'd just completed another purchase, this time with the mayor's wife. "And I can't believe they don't see me."

Hattie put her arm around her shoulder and squeezed. "I'm afraid people usually only see the surface, dear."

Anna smiled. "I for one am glad you looked deeper."

"Me too." She gave her another hug. "Do you have plans with Jeremy this afternoon? If you like I'll take over here and you can spend some time with your beau."

Anna's face flushed. "He's not my beau. We're just friends."

"Ah, well then, are you spending time with your *friend* this afternoon?"

She grinned wide and gave Hattie a nod, her face still flushed.

With a soft laugh, she waved the girl off. "Then you are free to go, dear. And have a good time."

It took only a second or two for Anna to disappear to freshen up, her step almost a skip. The bell over the door jangled, and Hattie turned to find the hotel manager. She cast him a bright smile, although he hadn't been all that pleased she'd not returned to the hotel as a regular paying customer, he had to realize she couldn't live there forever.

"What can I do for you, Mr. Gladstone?"

"My wife has been in here several times a week and not so casually mentioned the items you have for sale. I was wondering if you could show me what it is that has caught her eye."

"Of course. She has looked at the hat pins and I believe actually purchased one last week, but she does tend to return to the brooches. They are the latest rage."

"Are they terribly expensive?"

"The prices vary depending on the detail and the stones within, but these three are the ones she tends to examine the most."

He picked up each of the brooches and noted the price on the small tag tied to it by a string, and chose the one in the middle. "This one I think."

"Excellent choice," she said with a smile. "Not too expensive, not too flashy, and can be worn to church on Sunday. I know she'll be pleased."

"I hope so. It's our seventh anniversary next week and if I were to forget or choose poorly, I'd never hear the end of it."

They shared a chuckle as she placed the brooch in a box and wrapped it in paper. She finished with a piece of ribbon tied into a bow. It was a gift, after all, and not a simple bit of costume jewelry.

He handed her the money with his sincere thanks, then left with his surprise hidden in his pocket. Hattie couldn't contain her smile. She knew her emporium would be a success. Just a few items that would normally have to be had in a catalog, sight unseen, made her shop unique and profitable. Those that still held some grudge or thought her uncouth, never shopped there, but so many more did.

She turned to tidy the table behind the counter where

she'd wrapped Mr. Gladstone's gift when the door jingled again. Lifting her head, she was surprised to find yet another gentleman, one she didn't know. They did get them from time to time, but two in one day was saying something. She moved around the counter to where he stood examining the case where items for men were stored. Cigarette cases, upper end shaving supplies, and the like. The type of things the ladies purchased as gifts for their men.

"May I help you find something in particular? I'd be happy to pull out any of the items in the case."

He turned to look at her, his gaze flowing over her from head to toe with a somewhat surprised look on his face.

"Are you the owner?" he asked.

She decided he simply hadn't expected the shop to be run by a woman and let his rudeness go unchecked. "Yes I am. I'm Mrs. Baker. What can I do for you?"

"Don't you recognize me, Hortense?"

She took an unsteady step back. Only one man ever called her that, because he knew how much she detested the name. Even her own father never called her Hortense. It had been a family name, one that her parents felt obliged to give her, but they always called her Hattie.

She cleared her tight throat. "No, I'm sorry. Have we met?"

"I guess I've changed some, but I'd hoped you'd at least recognize your own husband."

Her blood ran cold as she took two more unsteady steps back. Shaking her head, she said, "My husband is dead."

"And yet here I stand."

She couldn't move, she couldn't think. It was

impossible, it couldn't be him. His clothes were a bit rough, not of the quality John would normally wear, and he sported a close beard, another thing John never did. He detested facial hair. No, it couldn't be him. She refused to believe it.

He moved to stand beside the table of fine linens and fingered an embroidered handkerchief. "Imagine my surprise to return home and find you gone, no house, no nothing. It wasn't too difficult to track you down." He pulled his idle gaze from the finery on the table to look at her. "But this? Not what I would've expected from someone of your social standing, but you always were…different."

"Get out," she said, her voice barely a whisper.

His taught lips pulled into a frightening grin. "Not until I get what's mine."

The way he looked at her struck an odd chord inside her. Something was different, something more than his clothes and beard…something not right.

Squaring her shoulders and mustering her courage, she tilted up her chin and stared him straight in the eye. "There's nothing here that's yours."

"Oh, I beg to differ, my dear devoted wife. You have my saloon and this shop, not to mention what was left to you, or should I say us, by your father. I only want what's rightfully mine. I'll be happy to take it in cash. Then you can continue on as you are. As if I was never here."

"I'll give you nothing!" No, this was wrong, he was wrong.

"Then I'll take it all."

This couldn't be happening, it was impossible, and yet his tone, almost evil, had sent a frightening shiver down Hattie's spine.

****

Colt had stood listening in the hallway, and with every word his heart dropped lower in his chest.

Married. She was still married. She hadn't lied to him, she'd truly believed her husband dead, but she was now and forever out of his reach. And yet, he could not, would not allow the scoundrel to blackmail her.

He pushed his shattered dreams to the side and entered the emporium. "I'm afraid you're mistaken, sir," he said. "Mrs. Baker not only won't give you any money, she cannot give you any money. The store and the saloon do not belong to her…or you. They belong to me."

The man's gaze narrowed as he looked between Hattie and Colt. "Well, well. This is unexpected. I never figured you the type to shack up with the first fat rat that would crawl into your bed."

Colt's jaw clenched. He would do whatever he could to make sure this man never bothered Hattie again— husband or no. "Either you leave right now, or I'll have to carry you out."

He looked Colt over, noted his side-arm, weighing his odds, then looked back to Hattie. "This isn't over. I'll have what's mine," he said, then stormed out, slamming the door behind him.

Hattie rushed to the door, threw the bolt and flipped the sign over to closed. She stood there with her hand on the knob and her forehead pressed to the door.

Her husband wasn't quite the fool Colt thought he was, but he would be back and with leverage to get what he wanted. Although legally Hattie could own property and work without her husband's consent, any wages she earned, any money she had would still be his to have and control in a court of law.

Anna slipped up beside him where he stood and elbowed him in the side. She pulled the revolver from the folds of her skirts and slipped it back into her pocket. "I came to see what the ruckus was about, but I see you handled it."

He cast her a half a grin.

With a nod toward Hattie, she said, "There's no time like the present for a second chance."

He shook his head as he gazed at Hattie still standing against the door her dead husband had just walked through.

"Someone once told me it wasn't every day you held a royal flush," Anna said. "Don't toss away a winning hand again, Colt. You love her, she loves you—simple. The rest will work itself out."

She turned and disappeared into the hall. His little girl had really grown up. This was his family. Not the one back in New York, the one he'd been born into. Here in Willow Bend with these people was where he belonged. He'd been such a fool.

His gaze returned to Hattie, and he crossed to where she stood, resisting the urge to put his arms around her. After all, she wasn't a widow any longer.

"Are you alright?" he asked.

She seemed to snap out of the daze she was in and lunged at him. Her arms flew around his neck, while her tear-stained face pressed against his chest, her soft sobs muffled by his coat.

"It's okay, sweetheart. I won't let him hurt you."

She continued to cry in his arms, so he guided her up to her room and onto the small settee in her parlor. He produced a handkerchief for her use, then went and got her a glass of water. "Do you need your medicine? Just tell me where it is and I'll get it for you."

She shook her head then dried her eyes and blew her nose. He took a seat beside her and slid his arm around her still shivering shoulders. "Come here," he said, and pulled her against his side. "It'll be okay. He won't get your store."

"But he looks so much like him," she said, her head resting against his shoulder.

"Like who?"

"Like John."

"Oh, sweetheart. It'll be alright," he said, knowing what a shock it must have been to see him after believing him dead for so long.

She pulled from his arms and sat up, as she wiped at her nose. "You don't understand. I mean he isn't John Baker, he's an imposter."

He felt his jaw go lax. "Excuse me?"

She took a deep breath and sat straighter, a gleam of the strong-willed woman he knew resurfacing. "I'm saying that man is an imposter."

Colt took her hand in his and gave it a soft pat. He didn't know quite how to handle this. "Sweetheart, you've just had a shock—"

"Stop patronizing me," she snapped and stood. She marched to the opposite side of the room, her fists on her tiny waist. "I'll admit it was, well, shocking, but I'm not having some sort of delusional episode. That man is not," she said, pointing toward the street, "I repeat most emphatically, he is not my husband, Jonathan T. Baker."

He sat forward on the settee his arms resting on his thighs. His lungs had finally begun to take in air after her firm declaration. She was still a widow. He wasn't in love with a married woman.

But he had to be sure. "Hattie, it's been years since you've seen him, and time changes a man. Are you absolutely sure he's not your husband?"

She sighed, her arms falling to her side. "Without question." She returned to sit by his side. "If he hadn't caught me so unawares, I would have been able to note several more things about him."

"Like what? What did you see that told you he wasn't John Baker?"

"His choice of attire, his facial hair, his mannerisms, the way he stands, the way he cocked his head while observing me."

"Hmm, all too small for noting in a court of law," Colt murmured. "It would be your word against his."

"Law? What do you mean?"

"My guess is, although he can't get his hands on the store or the saloon, he'll try and get your money. To do that, all he has to say is he's your husband. We can fight him in court, but we have to prove he isn't John Baker. No easy task since all your family and friends are gone, anyone who would've helped identify him. We've only your testimony against his."

"That was another clue," she said. "He didn't seem to be aware that Father had made sure he could never touch my inheritance. That man, that imposter, had included it in his *rightful due* list. John knew the details of what Father had done. He and Father's attorneys told him so to his face after he'd learned that John had only married me for money and how poorly he treated me."

"I think I would've liked your father," Colt said.

"And he would've liked you," she said, pressing her hand atop his.

Her shoulders sagged and she leaned back against

the cushions. "As it stands, the only money he could lay his hands on as my husband would be my earnings from the store. Although I should go down to the bank immediately and make sure that Mr. Fairfax is aware of this fraud. Still, there's not much there. I spent quite a sum stocking the store. And I've not requested any new funds from my inheritance of late."

Colt pressed his hand atop hers and lay his head back against the cushions beside hers. "There's time for that. And it wouldn't look good if you were to move a mass of funds to another account. It would appear in court that you intentionally tried to hide it from him, when by law it's his as well."

"He really isn't my husband, Colt. There are some things a woman can never forget. Mostly how the man she married looks at her, and that man didn't look at me the way John did. This man seemed, confused, almost surprised when he saw me. As if he'd never seen me before in his life."

He stroked her cheek with the backs of his fingers. "That's because he saw a beautiful woman."

A small grin slipped over her lips. "Through your eyes, I am. I see it when you look at me." She lifted her head and gave him a crooked grin. "But what, pray tell, has brought you home and are you staying?"

"You and yes." He slid his hand behind her head and brought her lips to his. With a gentle caress, he kissed her. "I was a fool to leave, to try and not want you," he whispered against her mouth.

"Why did you do it?" she whispered in return, as they shared a myriad of soft kisses between words. "What made you not want me anymore?"

He chuckled roughly. "Does this feel like I don't

want you?"

She grinned beneath his continued attentions to her delectable mouth. "Well, no. But you left and acted like you never wanted to see me again."

He pulled his mouth from hers and rested his forehead against hers on a sigh. "I'd overheard some of the gossip and I didn't like it. I didn't want them to hurt you, to shun you because of me, a gambler turned saloon owner living so close that we could carry-on in secret."

She cupped his cheek and pressed a kiss to his lips, soft and sweet. "Oh, Colt. I knew that sort of thing would be said, but I didn't care, and I don't care now. No amount of gossip, not even your absence is going to change how I feel. You are the man I want. You are the man I love."

He gazed into her eyes, unable to find the slightest of doubts hovering there. "I love you, Hattie. I never thought I'd ever say those words."

"Not even to your sweethearts in the past," she said, a teasing glint in her eye.

"I have never in my life said those words to anyone. Well," he chuckled. "My mother, of course. But never anyone else. Just you."

With a wide smile, she fell against him, her arms around his neck, and kissed him. He could feel her heart pounding in a passionate tattoo against his. He had to force himself to pull back before he would be unable to refrain from taking their heated kiss to the next level.

"We need to end this before it goes too far," he said.

"Define too far?"

"Hattie," he warned. "I'm just this close to picking you up and carrying you into your bedroom."

"Oh, I think that sounds wonderful," she said with a

sigh against his lips.

With a rough laugh, he pulled her arms from his neck. "And it would be, except for the fact that you we have an imposter to expose and we aren't married."

"I told you I don't care about that."

"I do. Now behave."

She fell back on the settee laughing, and he had to laugh with her. He was the one with questionable morals according to how society viewed him, while she was the proper widow from the upper classes. It was quite the turn of the table.

"Well, that's a good sign," Anna said, easing through the door. "Hope I'm not interrupting, but I could hear the laughter clear through the floor and wanted to make sure everything was okay."

"Oh, Anna, everything is wonderful," Hattie said.

"Uh-huh. Even though you've got a dead husband demanding his just dues?" She looked at Colt, her smile crooked. "I'm not even going to ask what you did to make her that happy. I'm sure you'll say I'm too young to know."

He stood and tweaked the tip of her nose. "Hell, Anna, you were born old, and no, that isn't how I made her happy. But I'm about to make her happier—I hope."

He dropped to his knee in front of where Hattie sat, and took her hand. She went stock still, her eyes wide.

"Hattie, will you marry me? I know I'm just a gambler, but I love you, and I want you—the three of us to be a real family. Now, I know that living next to a saloon isn't ideal, but we'll figure it all out. And we'll figure out this dead husband issue. I just don't want to go through another day knowing I could lose you to someone else. You're already the love of my life. Please.

Be my wife."

The silence lengthened as a tear ran down Hattie's cheek.

"Well, don't just sit there, say yes!" shouted Anna.

"Yes! Oh, yes!" She leapt from the settee into his open arms and cried happy tears, which he wiped away with his kisses.

Anna let out a shout. "Whoohoo!"

"What in blazes is going on up here?" Patty and Lila said, poking their heads through the door.

"They're gettin' hitched," Anna announced.

"Well, it's about damn time," Lila said.

"Yeah, you'd think Colt could've read that poker face on Hattie from the start, seeing as how he's a good gambler and all," Patty said.

"Just goes to show you, when the heart is involved, you just can't make sense of things," Lila said, as Anna escorted them back downstairs, leaving Hattie and Colt alone.

"Hattie, honey, there are some things you need to know about me," Colt said.

She pulled her lips from his, one lone brow arched. "If you tell me you're married already, I may just take that revolver of Anna's and shoot you."

"No, sweetheart, not married—not yet." He pressed a quick kiss to her lips. "But let's sit down and I'll explain."

Colt took her hands in his and looked her in the eye while he spoke, the more he said, the more Hattie felt vindicated that her assumptions about him were correct. She knew he was so much more than a gambler. She'd sensed it the day she met him, and the more they talked, she knew he'd been formally schooled, but she'd not begun to imagine how far.

"Are you, by chance, speaking of the Ambersons, as in Amberson, Cromely, and Smythe? The most prestigious law firm in New York, perhaps even the country?"

He sighed and bowed his head, his cheeks appearing a bit ruddy with a blush. Clearing his throat, he said, "Yes. That would be my family, and my father's law firm. I am, legally, Maximillian Coltrane Amberson. Third son of Ambrose and Marie Amberson."

"I see." She rose and crossed the room, a heavy weight lifting from her shoulders with every step. Colt would never marry for her money. His, or rather his family's money put her own wealth to shame. But would he want to return to society, to the upper classes where she was always so miserable?

"I know it's a lot to take in," he said. "I know it was a lie by omission, but you must understand why I did it. Please tell me you understand, Hattie."

She turned, a small smile on her lips. "I understand and I don't blame you for keeping such a thing secret." She let out half a laugh. "We've both had our share of them. My inheritance is put to shame by your family's money, but as you've already guessed, I am very well off."

"I know and I don't care."

She smiled then let the smile fall. "But Colt, I have to know something. Something I have to know before we marry."

He rose and crossed to her, taking her into his arms. "Of course, sweetheart. Ask me anything, anything at all."

"If your family asked you to, would you return to

New York. To that life?"

He smiled slow and shook his head. "No, Hattie. I left because it never suited me. I didn't like the types of cases I was forced to work on, the sometimes blatant use of power. Nor the soirees and ridiculous hobnobbing with the elite to garner more prestigious clients. I detested every moment of it. And I hate living in a big suffocating city. No, I would never return to that life."

"I know what you mean about the city. We have such fabulous sunsets here, the kind you can never see in New York. And those awful soirees. I had to play hostess a time or too, but my father needed me. He was the only reason I did it and he only did it when he had to."

"You know, if we'd stayed in New York, we may have actually met one day," he said.

"Possibly," she said. "Even then I think we would've found a friend in one another—a comradery of a sort."

"No doubt. I actually ran into my older brother while I was away. He told me of his upcoming nuptials and it made me want to go back, for just a split second. A place to belong, to be with family, however odious the work. But the idea died almost instantly, because in that same moment I realized I couldn't live my life without you. That all I would be doing is what my family has said I've done my whole life—run away. I'm not sure I agree with them, but I was running away from you, and I knew there was no place I could go, nothing I could do that would make me stop loving you."

"So, you ran back to me." Her heart filled to overflowing with his words.

"That I did. You and that brat of ours downstairs," he said with a chuckle.

"But what about the law? I've seen you reading countless legal texts and articles. Don't you miss being a lawyer?"

"I do, some days, but not there, not in that environment. If I do decide to practice law it will be here, on my own terms where I choose the clients. I did keep my license up to date, just in case."

She smiled. "Well then, Counselor, you have your first client. I will need proper representation to prove that my husband is indeed dead."

"And you will have it, Mrs. Baker, because I don't intend to lose you. Not now, not ever."

She kissed him with all her heart and soul, letting him know how she felt, because there were no words to convey the immense joy flowing like quicksilver through her veins.

"Hmm," he said, ending the kiss. "I think we'd better let everyone know to keep our betrothal a secret until this is all sorted out, however."

She let out a heavy sigh, knowing he was right. "Very well, but I refuse to go without kisses. I demand to have them regularly," she said with a grin.

He kissed her on the tip of the nose. "And have them you shall. Now, let's get downstairs and hope we can stop the gossip mill in time."

Hattie held fast to Colt's hand and followed him down to the saloon kitchen where everyone was gathered for their dinner. They explained the situation, for the most part, leaving out the bits about Colt's prestigious family, and everyone understood. Patty and Lila wanted to find the imposter and skin him alive, which warmed Hattie's heart, but Colt made it clear they were all to keep their distance, lest any type of interaction could be seen as coercion and possibly jeopardize the case.

As expected, the following morning, the sheriff paid Hattie a call at the emporium.

Chapter Nine

"What can we do for you, Sheriff?" Hattie asked, knowing full well why he was there.

Anna ran to fetch Colt.

"I've had a fella in my office this morning claiming to be your husband, Mrs. Baker. And I honestly ain't too sure how to handle this. He says you have to stop working here and you have to turn over your bank account. Seems Mr. Fairfax wouldn't give him so much as a penny."

Hattie couldn't refrain from letting out a deep and long-lasting breath. God bless Mr. Fairfax for truly listening to her.

The sheriff continued, "Now, I don't want to get caught in the middle of a marital dispute, and I don't know what to tell you legally." He grinned a bit sheepishly. "I'm afraid the most I do is lock up drunks and deal with rowdy cowpokes and handle small disputes."

"I understand, Sheriff. It isn't every day a dead man walks into your office."

"You got that right. But I know he's been here, and I expect he upset you some, and I'm sorry for that. He's a bit of a windbag, if you pardon me for saying so."

Hattie almost laughed aloud, which would be so improper in light of current events.

"But seeing as how he is your husband, ma'am, I

144

think you ought to do as he says."

"Matt, he has no right to tell her to stop working here, nor can he take command of her bank account," Colt said, coming through the hall doorway. "As of this minute," he said, handing him a stack of papers, "Mrs. Baker is declaring the man in question to be an imposter. She's bringing litigation against him for fraud, therefore anything he claims is nothing but words until a court settles the matter."

He turned to Hattie once Matt took the papers and gave them a look. "The Women's Property Act allows you to possess property and money, so even if he wins, he can't just have the whole account, but it could be argued that half of it is his if he is proven to be your husband."

She nodded at him, understanding her position legally. She's had to read numerous legal documents in her day and was fully aware of the changes occurring every day where women's rights were concerned. "And if he wins, which he won't because he most definitely is not my husband, I will sue for divorce. I refuse to have anything to do with the reprobate."

Colt cast her a sly wink, bringing a grin to her lips.

"Well, this makes things a might different," the sheriff muttered, as he looked up from the papers. "I'll see if I can get you on the judge's schedule so this thing can get sorted out quickly."

"Thanks Matt. And just to be clear, you know who owns this property, so I'm giving you fair warning that if he shows his face around here, I'm tossing him out."

"I understand. And Mrs. Baker, if he does show up or give you any trouble, you let me know. I don't cotton to harassment of a lady—wife or no."

She smiled at the long-legged man, so quiet and calm with a wicked grin and a true sense of honor. "Thank you, Sheriff. I am very appreciative of your help in this matter."

"My pleasure, ma'am. Colt, I'll let you know what the judge says."

With that he left and Hattie stepped back to lean against the counter, her heart racing in her chest.

"You okay?" Colt asked.

"Shaken I suppose. I still can't believe this is happening."

"Don't worry, sweetheart, we'll win this hands down."

"I hope you're right. I'd rather not have to divorce him. It would taint Anna, and I want her to have the best possible future."

A soft snort echoed from kitchen doorwary. "Taint me. Listen to yourself. You forget where I came from, Hattie," Anna said.

"Anna, it matters. What I do matters to your future."

The young woman shook her head. "My future is mine. I own it. You gave me that, you and Colt. You made me realize that I am in charge of my own life. And besides, I wouldn't want anything to do with someone that looked down on you no matter what you did or didn't do. They wouldn't be worth beans to me." She spun on her heels and went back inside the shop kitchen.

Hattie smiled, knowing she'd take out her anger at this whole nonsense on a batch of bread, or perhaps taffy, just like Hattie always did. She'd beat and pound on the mass, releasing her frustrations, until she felt better or the dough or candy was ruined.

"We've got quite a girl there, don't we, sweetheart?"

Colt said, slipping his hand in hers.

"That we do, my love. That we do."

****

It was only a matter of days before Hattie and Colt appeared before the judge. Apparently her imposter husband was so sure he'd win, he'd let the entire town know about it. Not only had he boasted success, he'd managed to charge up quite the sum at the hotel and the other saloon in town. Oddly enough, his boasting was about the only thing that resembled her dead husband.

Colt pulled out the chair in front of their appointed place in the courtroom for Hattie and leaned close to whisper in her ear. "I'm sorry the town's turned out for this, Hattie."

"It's not your fault. There hasn't been anything this exciting in town since I first arrived, I imagine."

Anna slipped her hand over Hattie's as she sat beside her. "It'll be okay. If anything, maybe this will make the naysayers see what a good person you are and stop being so snooty."

Hattie squeezed her hand in return with a grin.

The clerk called the session to order, but it took Judge Hartfield's banging his gavel to quiet the room, his surprise at the assembly evident on his weathered features.

"Mr. Coltrane, please state your case," the judge said.

Colt began the proceedings with such professional aplomb Hattie had to force herself not to smile, she was so proud of him. Her father would've truly adored Colt, of that she had no doubt, and somehow felt that he may have even had a hand in bringing them together. A silly thought, but it felt true, never-the-less.

Anna squeezed her hand beneath the table and cast her a conspiratorial wink.

"Your honor, this man claims to be one John T. Baker, formerly of New York. Husband to Hortense Little Baker. Mrs. Baker received this death certificate, Your Honor, along with her husband's personal belongings in March of 1873. It was reported that John T. Baker was killed on the night of February twentieth in a saloon in Dodge City over a game of cards." Colt handed the certificate to the judge. "Mrs. Baker has stated in this affidavit that this man is not her husband." He handed the affidavit to the judge.

Judge Hartfield nodded and examined the certificate and Hattie's statement. "Thank you, Counselor." The judge turned to the imposter. "You've heard the complaint, sir. What is your response?"

Not very formal, in Hattie's opinion, but Willow Bend was a small town and he was a small-town judge, who, most likely, just wanted to get on with things.

"I am John T. Baker, Your Honor, whether my wife likes it or not," he said.

The judge sighed heavily. "Well, Mr. Baker, regardless of your word, there is a death certificate bearing your name," he said, holding up the paper. "You will have to provide some proof as to your identity before I can come to any decision regarding this case."

"I have a witness, Your Honor," the imposter said, waving a hand to the man beside him. "Doctor Williams here will vouch for me."

Judge Hartfield waved the clerk over to the doctor. "Swear him in, George, and put him on the stand."

The man crossed the room to the chair beside the judge and placed his hand on a bible and swore to tell the truth, then sat down.

"There's something strange about that man," Anna whispered. "Something familiar."

"Maybe he's been here before," Hattie whispered.

"Whoever he is, he poses a big problem," Colt murmured.

"Now then, Doctor, can you vouch for this man?"

"I can, sir." The stranger cupped the lapel of his jacket and cleared his throat. "There was quite a ruckus that involved several men that night in Dodge City, many of whom were brought to me with various wounds, but it was not John Baker who was killed. It was an acquaintance of Mr. Baker, who had died. Mr. Baker, however, had been gravely wounded and remained unconscious for several days, unaware of his friend's fate. The authorities merely confused the two men, who had been sharing a room at the hotel, when they collected his things. It was simply a situation of mistaken identity."

Hattie's heart dropped and her stomach twisted and churned. She thought she might be sick. How was she to win against such a story? She knew that man wasn't her husband. Watching him now, noting his every movement and facial expression, she had absolutely no doubt that he was a fraud. It would seem she'd have to divorce the man after all.

Colt, squeezed Hattie's hand beneath the table then rose. "Your Honor, if I may ask a few questions?"

"Proceed."

"Doctor, your name is not the one on the death certificate."

"That's correct. As I said, there were many injured that night. I tended to Mr. Baker here. I was not made aware of the mistake until after he awoke."

"And yet you made no effort to have the certificate corrected or notify his family."

"I let the attending doctor know of the confusion. It was his place to make the correction, not mine."

"I see. And how is it you came to be in Willow Bend at this time, Doctor?"

"Why I, um, came along with Mr. Baker."

"I see. So, Mr. Baker had cause to believe that his wife wouldn't recognize him."

"Well—no. That's—that's preposterous," he blustered and stammered.

"No more questions, Your Honor."

"You may return to your seat, Doctor," the judge said, then looked to the imposter. "Mr. Baker, in knowing that there had been a mistake, did you make an attempt to notify your wife of the error?"

"No, sir. We weren't on the best of terms and I figured the doctor had done it," he said, his voice low.

"And do you, Mrs. Baker, after hearing the doctor's testimony, still swear this man is not your husband?" the judge asked.

"Yes, Your Honor, I do."

Judge Hartfield sat back in his chair with a sigh. "It seems I have a difficult decision here. One I don't take lightly, but dead men can't talk, and yet here he sits."

"Oh, no. It can't be," Anna whispered.

"It's alright, dear. I'll just divorce him," Hattie whispered and clasped Anna's hand.

"No, it's not that." Anna grabbed Colt's arm. "Call me as a witness."

He shook his head with a frown.

"Just do it," she whispered harshly.

"Your honor, I would like to call a witness," Colt said.

The judge nodded with a frown.

"I call Miss Anna Baker to the stand."

Anna crossed to the chair, swore to tell the truth then sat down.

Colt cast Hattie a baffled look before approaching Anna. Hattie shrugged her shoulders, leaving him wondering what Anna was up to. She couldn't be anything more than a character witness, which really wasn't much help. But at this point, he was willing to try anything to win this case.

"Will you please state your name and your relationship to Mrs. Baker, please?" he asked Anna.

"Anna Baker. I am Mrs. Baker's daughter."

The imposter jumped to his feet. "She's lying! We have no children!"

Judge Hartfield pounded his gavel. "Be seated, sir. You'll have your chance to say your peace."

Anna cleared her throat. "Sorry, Judge, he's right. Hattie has no children. I'm adopted." With that, she shot the imposter such a look, Colt had to hide his grin.

"And has Mrs. Baker been a good mother to you, Miss Baker?" Colt asked.

"She's been an angel. If it weren't for Hattie—and a few others that know me—I don't know what my life would've been like." She half waved Colt away and turned to the judge. "You see Judge, when I met Hattie and Colt here, I was nothing but—well, everyone in town called me orphan trash."

"Anna, don't," Hattie said with a gasp.

"It's alright, Hattie. I may as well tell it. Sooner or later, someone will figure it out, and that'd be kind of embarrassing."

A tear came to Hattie's eye and Colt had to swallow hard himself.

"Continue, Miss Baker," the judge said.

"Well, you see when I was about ten years old, my paw up and left me. Took off in the middle of the night cause he owed a few too many people money."

"He abandoned you," the judge said.

"Yes. But a few here in town were kind enough to make sure I was taken care of. Like Mr. Cochran, the blacksmith, and Colt here and Mr. Hanson over at the saloon."

The judge's face scrunched up and then he grinned. "Are you telling me you're Canna?"

Anna's grin spread from one ear to the other. "Yep, it's me, Judge. I didn't think you'd recognize me either. Seems no one does," she said, with a glance to half the town sitting in the audience gasping and whispering.

The judge pounded his gavel. "Quiet in the courtroom! I'll clear this hall if I have to."

"What has this got to do with me?" the imposter yelled from his chair.

"Be quiet! You'll have your say, I said." He turned back to Anna with a smile. "Go on, Canna—I mean Miss Baker."

"Thank you, Judge. Well, now that it's out there and everyone is aware of who I was and who I am now, they all know that Hattie is an angel to be sure. Not many folks would do what she done—did for me. She and Colt. They're good people, Judge. The best, and I know for a fact that Hattie would never lie about this man not being her husband."

"I have to agree with you, Miss Baker on Mrs.

Baker's character, but I'm afraid that isn't enough to prove this man is an imposter."

"Yeah, well, I figured that, and frankly I wasn't going to say anything about me being who I was and all. Didn't seem to be a need. But then I recognized the doctor there, and Judge, he ain't no doctor."

"That's a lie," Doctor Williams said, jumping to his feet with the imposter right beside him.

The judge pounded his gavel again and both men sat back down with a scowl.

"Why do you say that, Miss Baker? How do you know this gentleman?" the judge asked.

"Cause that's Ambrose Baggs, my paw."

The courtroom burst wide open with that, and the judge nearly broke his gavel trying to calm the room.

"Your Honor," Colt called over the ruckus. "I move that the witness testimony be dismissed."

Judge Hartfield rubbed his jaw and thought on it a bit, while Colt waited, not liking the look in the old man's eye.

"Miss Baker, how long has it been since you've seen your father?" the judge asked.

"About five years. Took a few minutes for me to see through his fancy clothes and the beard, but that's him, Judge. I'm sure of it."

He looked to Colt. "Counselor, if you can find another witness to testify that this is Ambrose Baggs, I'll throw out his testimony." He glanced at Baggs and narrowed his gaze. "And I'll have him thrown in jail for child abandonment, impersonating a doctor, and perjury."

"Yes, Your Honor. With pleasure," Colt said.

Baggs visibly paled as he sank down in his seat. The

imposter didn't look too pleased either.

"Case in recess until after lunch!" The judge pounded the gavel and rose from his chair. "Miss Baker," he said, turning to Anna as she stood. "I'm very glad things worked out for you."

"Thanks, Judge. Sorry I won't be around to do your errands anymore," she said with half a laugh.

He grinned. "You know why I had you running all over town."

"Yes, sir, I do. You're an old softy at heart, just like the others who were looking out for me."

He cast her a wink then left the courtroom.

Hattie rushed to Anna while Colt and the sheriff were doing their best to keep half the town from mobbing them both. Some saying they'd known all along, others apologizing for thinking ill thoughts of Hattie, others just wanting to congratulate Anna in her good fortune, it was pure chaos.

"I need to get you two out of here," Colt grumbled, guiding them to the back door behind the judge's bench.

He escorted them all the way back to The Golden Lady and around to the kitchen. He noticed Hattie being uncommonly quiet the entire way.

"Why don't the two of you have some lunch, rest a bit, while I try and find those witnesses," he said as they entered.

Hattie merely nodded.

"Sweetheart, it will be alright. Anna will give me a list of people and I'll try and round them all up."

"Yes. Yes, I know. I think I'll lie down for a bit. Before lunch." She left the kitchen and went down the hall toward the emporium and their apartment above.

"I don't like the way she looks," Anna said. "This

whole thing has her upset more than she's saying."

"I agree, but we're doing all we can. So, who do I need to find?"

"Mr. Cochran and Mr. Gladstone, and even though I don't think he'd be much help, old man Jenkins." She sliced up some bread and meat as she spoke. "Paw and he were pretty tight for a spell, but he never paid his bill at the hotel restaurant and when he took off, he took a horse and tack that he'd leased from Mr. Cochran."

Anna handed Colt a sandwich.

"Thanks." He ate the thing in three bites, eager to get those witnesses, then nearly choked at the sound of a loud bang.

He and Anna exchanged glances, then realized what it was. "Hattie," they said in unison, and took off up the stairs to the apartment.

Colt burst through the door of her bedroom to find her writhing on the floor. He froze at the horrible sight, but only for a moment before falling to his knees beside her.

"Hold her arms and legs so she doesn't hurt herself!" Anna said. "I'll hold her head."

Colt did as he was told with tears hanging in his eyes. He felt useless, unable to stop the seizure, hurting inside more than he'd ever hurt before because he couldn't help the woman he loved. He hoped and prayed with all his heart he wouldn't lose her, not now, not when they were just beginning.

After what felt like an eternity, Hattie fell still then moaned.

"Hattie, we've got you. It's okay, we're here," Anna said. "Get her on the bed, Colt so I can make her more comfortable while you fetch the doc."

Colt gently lifted her in his arms and pressed a kiss to her forehead. "I'm here, sweetheart. You're going to be okay."

Hattie moaned and her eyelids fluttered, but she never regained full consciousness.

"I'll send the doctor then go look for our witnesses. She needs this over now more than ever. If we lose the case, her husband can have her committed."

Anna gasped as she took off Hattie's shoes. "He'd do that?"

"Without a doubt. If she's unable to defend herself and file for a divorce, he has full control." Colt stroked Hattie's cheek then pressed a kiss to her brow. "I'll be back as soon as I can, sweetheart."

"But what about the judge?" Anna asked. "Can you finish this without either of us there?"

Colt crossed to the door. "I'll let him know that the strain has made her ill and you're by her side. There shouldn't be any reason for him to delay with all the testimony complete." He glanced one last time at Hattie, still unconscious.

"She'll be alright. This is the worst I've seen, but she'll be alright."

"She has to be," he muttered, then rushed to get the doctor.

Chapter Ten

The courtroom was overflowing with townsfolk, news of what had happened about Anna being Canna having spread like wild fire. Colt's frantic race for the doctor, then for the witnesses he needed to identify Baggs, had the whole town turned on its head.

He shouldered his way inside the courtroom as the judge was taking his seat. The fake John Baker was seated to the right as before, but the eye witness to the man's resurrection was nowhere to be seen.

Colt lay his satchel on the table then approached the bench. "Your Honor, I'm afraid that my client is indisposed at the moment."

The judge's brows rose, obviously waiting for further explanation. Colt didn't wish to reveal too much in public, not knowing what the judge would say to the town. Hattie's illness was private and he didn't want awful rumors circulating about her, so he proceeded with caution.

"She has an underlying condition, sir, and with the strain from the proceedings she has become quite ill. Anna and the doctor are with her at present, but I'm afraid she's unable to leave her sick bed."

"I see. I'm sorry to hear that, Counselor. But we've heard her testimony, so we shall proceed. I may need to call on Canna—I mean Miss Baker before we're finished here, however."

"I understand, sir. I have someone to act as a runner if she is needed." With that Colt returned to his place and waited for the judge to call the room to order.

He banged on the gavel and gave instructions to the room to come to order, then turned to the defendant. "Mr. Baker, your eye witness does not appear to be present."

"I'm sure he's just delayed, Your Honor." But Baker didn't look convinced of his own words.

As the judge was preparing to make a statement, there was a disturbance in the back of the room near the door, and within a few seconds, the sheriff came through the crowd carrying one Ambrose Baggs by the scruff of his neck.

"Found him trying to catch the afternoon train, Judge," Matt said.

"There's no need to man handle me, sir. I was only inquiring about the schedule," Baggs sputtered.

"From inside the passenger car?" the sheriff asked, and placed the man in his seat.

The judge pounded his gavel to quiet the room once more, while Colt did all he could not to hide his satisfied grin. The eye witness' testimony on more than shaky ground without others to swear to his identity.

"Counselor, do you have your witnesses ready? I think this needs to move along," the judge said.

"I do, Your Honor." Colt called Mr. Cochran to the stand and asked him if he believed the man beside Mr. Baker to be Ambrose Baggs. He didn't want to waste any more time. He wanted this sham to be over so he could get back to Hattie.

"Well. I think it's Baggs, but I just can't swear by it."

Colt felt his stomach drop. This wasn't how he

expected this to go. He was certain Anna knew her own father, he had absolutely no doubt the man was Baggs, but he feared that no one else would claim the same.

"I'm sorry, Colt. I just ain't sure."

With a grim sigh, he nodded.

"That's alright Mr. Cochrane. You've told the truth," the judge said. "And that's what matters here. "You may step down. Do you have others, Counselor?"

"Yes, Your Honor. I call Mr. Gladstone, to the stand."

There was a flurry of noise in the back of the room, and the judge repeated the call, but instead of Gladstone, old man Jenkins shoved his way through the crowd.

"Where is he?" he demanded. "Where's that shifty-eyed snake?" he yelled.

He stepped free of the crowd and spied Baggs seated to the right, then lunged for him. "I want my money, you scheming low life!"

The sheriff had to pull Jenkins off of Baggs before he killed the man, while one of his deputies kept Baggs from retaliating.

The judge pounded his gavel until it nearly broke. "Jenkins! Calm yourself!"

The room settled somewhat, but only so everyone could hear what would happen next.

"I want my money, Judge!" Jenkins waved his boney finger toward Baggs. "That slimy critter done stole more than fifty dollars from me!"

"That slimy critter being who?" the judge asked.

"Why that there's Ambrose Baggs! I'd know the rattle snake anywhere!" With that, Jenkins lunged again, but the sheriff was ready to keep them separated.

"He's lying, Your Honor! I've never seen this man

before in my life," Baggs retorted.

"It seems we have one for and one against," the judge muttered as he rubbed his brow.

Mr. Gladstone made his way through the crowd and took a stand next to Colt. "No sir, Your Honor. That's Baggs, I'd swear it on a stack of bibles that's him. And he owes me twenty dollars."

The shouts and voices of the crowd were too much for the judge's gavel, so he just gave up. More and more people were shouting it was Baggs and that they'd swear to it, and that he owed them all money.

"Ambrose Baggs, you're hereby charged with practicing medicine without a license, perjury, and whatever all these other charges are about," the judge shouted over the din with a wave of his gavel.

Now caught in the middle of his lies, the eye witness to Baker's resurrection, turned on his companion in an attempt to save his own skin. "I never did any practicin'! He promised ten percent of her money if I swore he was John Baker! He made up the lie, not me."

The fake John Baker jumped to his feet. "He's lying, Your Honor! He swore to me he was the doctor who tended me. I'm just as much a victim here!"

The judge tried again to bring the room to order.

"Your Honor, if I may!" Colt shouted, holding up a hand of papers.

That got everyone's attention, although the room still hummed with whispers, they were able to proceed.

"Continue, Counselor," the judge said.

"Mr. Baggs said that the defendant promised him a percentage of Mrs. Baker's money. Her inheritance, I presume is to what he's referring. I have here sworn affidavits from Mrs. Baker's attorneys that John T. Baker was made well aware of the fact that he would never receive a dime of her father's estate. That even if John Baker should survive her, all monies from her father's estate would never go to her husband."

Colt placed the affidavits on the stand. He'd expected to use them later if the case was to go in the defendant's favor. The man, whom he knew was not Hattie's husband, wouldn't argue with a quick divorce once he realized he wouldn't receive a single penny of her inheritance.

"It's a lie!" The fake John Baker rushed the stand to see the evidence for himself. "It can't be true," he muttered, looking over the papers.

"It would seem you went through all this for nothing, young man," the judge said lowly, and waved the sheriff over to take him into custody.

Matt took the befuddled fake Baker out the door with his deputy hauling Baggs behind.

The judge pounded his gavel amid the commotion and declared the case closed and the fake Baker under arrest for fraud and perjury.

Colt went back to his satchel to gather his things as quickly as possible so he could get the news back to Hattie.

"Counselor," the judge called. "I think Willow Bend could use a good lawyer full time. I hope you consider putting away the cards and hanging out a shingle."

He smiled at Judge Hartfield. "I think you might have something there, Judge."

He ran back to the emporium as fast as he could, his heart racing with the good news. When he bounded into the kitchen everyone was there and all eyes were wide and watching him.

He smiled wide. "We won, and they're both in jail." His face fell a bit. "I'm sorry Anna. Your father—"

"Is right where he belongs, if you ask me." She smiled and nodded to the hall. "She's awake, go tell her, then maybe she'll get some rest."

With a quick kiss to his daughter's brow, he bounded through the hall, up the stairs, and into Hattie's room. She was lying down, but her head turned the minute he entered.

"What happened?" she asked, her voice faint with fatigue.

"We won," he said, and moved to sit by her on the bed. He stroked her face with the backs of his fingers then pressed a kiss to her forehead. "It's all over, they're both in jail."

"Oh, thank goodness," she said, a weary sigh escaping her lips. "What about Anna? Is she upset about her father?"

"She's glad he's in jail. Now you need your rest. You have a wedding to plan, so you need to close your eyes and get all the rest you can." He smiled down at her soft smile as her lids slid closed, and pressed a kiss to her cheek.

He rose and moved to the door and paused at the sound of her soft voice.

"I love you," she said.

"And I love you. Now sleep," he said, and closed the door behind him.

Epilogue

Hattie took Colt's arm as he guided her out the back door of the kitchen. "Where are we going?"

"I told you, it was a surprise."

She laughed softly. "Colt, I don't need any more surprises. You're spoiling me."

"A man is supposed to spoil his betrothed."

"Well, after tomorrow, I'll be your wife, and you can stop—um—slow down on the surprises," she said, a cat-in-cream smile on her lips. She didn't want him to stop altogether. After all, what woman didn't like surprises from her husband. A new hat, a new dress, new fancy cash register for the emporium, the list went on and on. She'd never been so happy.

The only sad item was Anna's beau. Jeremy hadn't come to see her in days, not since she told the entire town who she was. It broke Hattie's heart to see her sad, but the girl repeated many times, that if he couldn't handle her past, then he wasn't worth a hill of beans.

"So, my surprises have been worth having, eh?"

"You know how much I love them all. But you are setting a precedent," she said with a grin. "You'll have to keep topping one after another, and sooner or later, you're going to find yourself in a pickle."

He laughed and pulled her to a stop along Willow Road where many of the townsfolk lived. It was a pleasant part of town, all trees and lawns. He turned her to face him. "Then this will be the last for a little while, I promise," he said, and pressed a quick kiss to the tip of her nose. Taking her hand, he turned and ushered her through a small gate surrounding a lovely green yard, then stopped at the foot of the stairs to a large white house.

"Who lives here?" she asked.

"We do. If you want to."

Her voice caught in her throat as she looked up at the man who held her heart.

"We both know that we can't live over the emporium, there's not enough room for all three of us, and we certainly can't live at the saloon, and we definitely will not be sleeping in separate beds, you in the apartment and me in the saloon, so I bought us a house. I didn't want to start our new life together without a proper bed for the newlyweds and a proper room for our daughter. But if you don't like it, I can sell it just as easily and buy something else. Or if you want, we can build or we can—"

She pressed her hand to his lips, silencing his hurried speech. "I love you and I love this house."

With a smile, he lowered his head and kissed her, sending her head into a dizzying whirl, then she realized it wasn't just his kiss. He'd literally swept her off her feet and was striding up the porch steps.

"Colt, what are you doing? The neighbors!"

"Can watch a man carry his wife over the threshold."

"But we're not married yet," she said, laughing as he nudged the door open.

"All the more luck to be had by carrying you over the threshold twice," he said, and pecked a quick kiss to her lips as he crossed into the wide foyer.

"Oh, this is beautiful," she said, as he lowered her to her feet.

She hurried to the parlor, holding in her squeal of glee. It was nothing compared to the large house she had in New York, but it was theirs and it was all she needed or wanted. Light and airy, with windows everywhere to let in breezes and the sunshine. Nothing like the dark imposing façade of her old house in New York.

He came up behind her and slipped his arms around her waist. "Do you really like it?"

She clasped her hand over his arms, as tears filled her eyes. "I do. I truly do."

"Is it safe to come in yet?" Anna's voice called from the front porch. "I wouldn't want to interrupt anything naughty."

Colt let out a bark of laughter. "Come in, brat!"

"You told her where we were going?" Hattie asked.

"I did, but under duress. The nosey little bloodhound found out what I'd done, and of course she wanted to see our new home too."

Laughing, Hattie turned in his arms and kissed him on the cheek, then stepped into the foyer just as Anna came through the door. "What do you think, dear?"

Anna's mouth hung open for a minute then focused on Hattie. "Is it okay with you, Hattie?"

"I think it's wonderful."

With a shout of glee, Anna hugged her. "So do I!" Then she took off like a shot, her skirts pulled up beyond her knees and bolted up the stairs. "I've got to see my room!"

"The biggest one is ours," Colt called after her, as he slid his arms around Hattie's waist.

****

The wedding went off without a hitch and they held a big bash in the yard of their new house. A wire had arrived from Colt's parents with congratulations and asking them when he would be bringing his new bride and daughter to New York for a visit. Colt made no promises and just replied soon.

By the end of the celebration, a chill began to blow in and they knew the summer was coming to a close. What a wild three months it had been. From gambler, to saloon owner, to husband and father, to—well, to family. He couldn't be a happier man.

The guests finally gone, Colt did his best to hide his eagerness in wanting to retire. After all, they still had a daughter living with them. But he knew Hattie wished the night would hurry up and fall as well.

Sitting on the front porch swing, they watched the sun dip lower in the sky. Hattie lay her head against his shoulder and sighed.

"Happy?" Colt asked.

"Gloriously happy," she replied. "You?"

He chuckled. "The only thing that could make me happier is for that sun to hurry up and set."

She smacked his chest. "Hush, Anna might hear you."

"Sweetheart, she knows all about the birds and the bees."

"I know, but it just seems so—so—oh I don't know. Uncouth."

"You are blushing, my dear wife."

She grinned and gave him a playful shove. "Stop teasing me."

As he tightened his arm around her, Anna stepped

onto the porch. "Well, all the dishes are done and everyone's gone home." She sat in the rocking chair beside them. "It sure was a pretty wedding." She fingered the delicate lace of her dress, the one Hattie had especially made for her to be her maid of honor. She had a feeling Anna might actually sleep in the thing, she'd been so over the moon about it.

"Yes, it was perfect," Hattie said.

"I hope mine is like that—someday, when I get hitched, I mean," Anna said.

"Anyone in particular, brat?" Colt asked.

She cast him a look, then shook her head. "No, but someday someone will come along. Look how long it took for you two to find one another. The way I figure it, there's a boy for every girl. I just have to keep my eyes open."

"I think someone has come calling already," he said, nodding toward the front gate where a nervous Jeremy Davis stood, twisting his cap.

Colt waved the young man over. The boy swallowed hard and came through the gate. He closed it behind him then crossed to the foot of the porch, still twisting his cap in his hands.

"What can we do for you, Jeremy?" Colt asked. Hattie held in her giggle, it wasn't nice to laugh at the poor boy's discomfort, but he deserved to be uncomfortable after leaving Anna wondering for so many days.

"I wanted to congratulate you on your wedding, sir and Mrs. Baker. I mean Coltrane."

"It's Amberson," Anna said, a faint growl in her voice.

"Right. Um—Amberson. Guess it'll take some time

to get used to the change," he said with a nervous chuckle.

"Thank you, Jeremy. Yes, I suppose there have been a lot of changes around here lately," Hattie said, casting Anna a look, but she smirked in return.

She wasn't fooling anyone, she liked the boy, but she was obviously determined to make him squirm a bit before forgiving him.

"Yes, ma'am. A right many." He looked at Anna, his gaze almost pleading.

"I think this is where we exit, sweetheart," Colt said. "You're welcome to stay and visit with Anna for a spell, Jeremy. But only for a few minutes. It's getting late," he said, using his best father's voice that had Anna looking at him like he'd grown another head.

Holding in their laughter at the young folks' expense, Hattie and Colt went inside to leave them alone, but the pair lingered in the foyer to listen. They couldn't help themselves.

"Anna, I want to say—that is—ah, heck. I'm sorry," Jeremy said.

"Sorry for what?" Anna replied, her tone cold.

"You mean you ain't mad?"

"Mad? What would I have to be mad about?"

"Well, that I hadn't come to call in a spell."

"Oh that. Frankly, I hadn't noticed. I've been awfully busy. Then of course there are all the tea parties I've attended lately. I met Dillon Fairfax at one just the other day. You know, the banker's son? He's home from college."

"Why that little—" Colt whispered.

Hattie pressed her fingers to his lips. "Hush, I want to listen."

"Oh. Yeah. I know Dillon. He's—um—he's okay, I reckon. Like I said, I wanted to apologize and all, and well, I guess I'll be goin' then."

Hattie peeked through the sidelight next to the front door and saw the young man turn, his head hanging low.

"I hope she doesn't leave it this way," Colt said.

"Neither do I. I've met Dillon, he's a bit of a snob."

"Not the one for our girl, then, eh?"

She shook her head as she watched the young man make his way down the stone path toward the gate. It was such a sad thing to watch.

"There's plenty of wedding cake left," Anna called after him. "If you'd like to stay and have some."

Jeremy turned, a small smile on his face. "I'd like that a lot."

"Come back to the kitchen, and we can have some buttermilk to go with it."

"Ooops," Hattie whispered, and Colt snagged her hand and they bolted into the parlor before the two came through the door. They quickly took a seat and pretended to each be reading. However, Hattie's book was upside down and her spectacles were nowhere to be seen.

Anna noted the false scene instantly with a roll of her eyes, then lead Jeremy to the kitchen.

"We've been discovered, sweetheart," Colt said with a chuckle.

"I'm afraid so."

"Well, I think it's safe for us to retire. I trust Jeremy," he said.

"So do I."

He rose and took her hand and lead her up the stairs. "Even if I didn't trust the boy, Anna would likely shoot him if he did anything she didn't like," Colt said.

With a laugh, Hattie agreed.

Colt pulled her to a stop at the end of the hall before their bedroom. "Well, Mrs. Amberson? Are you ready to embark on a new life with me?"

She tipped up on her toes and kissed him soundly. "More than anything, Mr. Amberson."

With a wide smile, Colt swept her off her feet, carried her over the threshold, and kicked the door soundly shut with his foot. The night was only just so long, and they had a lot of loving to do before sunrise.

Other books by Jo Barrett

Thank you for purchasing
this publication of The Wild Rose Press, Inc.
For questions or more information
contact us at
info@thewildrosepress.com.
The Wild Rose Press, Inc.
www.thewildrosepress.com

CPSIA information can be obtained
at www.ICGtesting.com
Printed in the USA
BVHW090629130722
641930BV00009B/686